REDEEMED

Andréa Joy

Redeemed
Andréa Joy

Copyright © 2020 by Andréa Joy

ISBN 978-1-9992413-4-6

Cover Design by: Raven Designs

Edited by: Nikki Holt Sexton

AUTHOR NOTE

If you're coming straight into *Redeemed* from *Cursed* you can skip the prologue. However, if it's been a while since you've read book 1, the prologue is the last chapter of *Cursed*.

Even though this story takes place in Toronto, Canada, the author has taken some creative liberties with locations, street names, and buildings within the book.

Happy reading :)

Andréa Joy

DEDICATION

To *BookTok After Dark*.
Thank you for all the laughs. Here's
to many more late night chats :)

Andréa Joy

TO LOVE AT ALL IS TO
BE VULNERABLE.

- C.S. Lewis

Andréa Joy

CARLO

October...

THE CABIN AND the driveway leading it up to are pitch black. I can't see anything outside the headlights of the Uber I had to call to bring me up here. When the car stops outside the cabin, I grab my overnight bag from the back and thank the driver before walking up to the front door. The driver doesn't even wait for me to be safely inside before backing down the driveway as fast as he drove up it. I ring the doorbell and wait. But nothing happens. I don't hear anything going on on the other side of the door either. I pull out my phone and turn on the flashlight and then head around the side of the cabin toward the back. Tiki torches light the perimeter of the backyard and lead a path down to the woods. I shudder thinking about the last time I ventured in there and that brings up memories of the man who attacked me down the street from the guys' house.

"Little Lamb!" Kane hollers from where the guys are seated around a bonfire. They're all dressed in the same dark jeans and hoodie. "You came!"

I giggle and drop my bag beside the log Jagger is sitting on and sit down beside him. "Hey, babe," he says, throwing an arm around my shoulders and drawing me into him. I melt against him when he plants a soft kiss on my forehead. *What is it about girls and forehead kisses?*

"You made it," Hunter grins from directly across the fire with Wolf at his side.

"Wouldn't miss it. I've missed you guys these past two weeks."

Happy smiles and grins at seeing me, turn forced and suddenly none of them will look me in the eyes.

"So," I say, trying to break the tension. "What's the plan for tonight?"

Wolf chuckles, reaching down into the cooler beside him and pulling out a bottle of rum. "Now, we drink, roast hot dogs, and make as many s'mores as our hearts desire."

I laugh, taking the bottle from Jagger when it comes its way to us. "I can toast to that," I say, holding up the bottle in a mock salute before taking a shot straight from it.

I've lost track of how many times we've passed the bottle around, but it seems like it gets me to faster and faster every time. Or maybe it's become permanently attached to my hand and I haven't been passing it along like I should? I shrug. Oh well, there loss. My stomach feels all warm and my head is all soft and flowy, and I'm definitely drunk.

"Truth or dare?" Jagger nudges my arm and I almost go tumbling off the log. He laughs and catches me by my arm. "Shit. You're cut off, Little Lamb." He pries the bottle from my hand, but honestly I'm happy to give it up. I don't remember rum going to my head this fast before.

"Ummmm, dare," I say, drawing the m out way more than necessary.

"We dare you to say yes," Hunter says. I squint at him through the orangey-red flames of the fire.

"Yes to what?"

"Do you want to play a game?" One of them says, but I can't figure out which one. Their voices are all blurring together at this point. It's probably about time that I call it a night and go snuggle into Hunter's bed in the cabin.

"We'll even give you a heads start." Someone else says.

Then I'm being hauled to my feet. Something is being shoved in my face but my vision is so blurry that it's hard to tell what it is. I blink once… twice… three times before the object becomes clear. Almost like a cold bucket of water is being dumped on my head, I'm instantly sober.

"Jagger, what are you doing?" Each of my breaths come faster than the one before it as I look between the four men who are now standing in a line in front of me. All with the same cold, dead look on their faces and in their eyes. It's a look I've never seen on them before, but one that terrifies me. I start to back up, consciously aware that with every step back I take, I get closer to the forest and further away from the cabin.

"Run." This comes from Kane. With one last look at all of them, I heed his warming and turn tail and run into the dark forest.

Leaves and fallen branches crunch and break on the forest floor under running footsteps. Blood rushes in my ears and I quickly glance back, but I don't see anyone. It's dark. The sun having set hours ago already. The front of my sneaker gets caught on something and I flail as I hit the ground hard on my knees. Pain, hot and fast slashes across my cheek and knees, but I don't give it another thought. I can't. Quickly, I scramble up again, kicking off the other shoes and try to ignore the way sticks and stones dig into the bottoms of my feet with each quick step. The thin socks I threw on are doing nothing to protect them. I have to get out of here. I have to get back home and tell my mom that I love her. Loud cackles sound nearby and I pick up speed, veering off the hiking path. I refuse to die here. In this forest. By the hands of the men I once thought I loved.

"Do you want to play a game?"

"We'll even give you a head start."

Their words from a few minutes ago echo through my head. Right before one of them shoved a gun in my face and told me to run. I knew they could be monsters. I just never thought that I'd be the one running from them.

"Beware."

"Beware."

"Beware."

"Beware."

The word echoes around me like they've got me surrounded but I still can't see them in the dark.

"Beware of the dark for that's where the monsters lurk."

I scream and fall back on my butt in the dirt when someone lands in front of me in a crouch before he straightens to his full height. My heart lurches. I almost told them I loved them that morning we all woke up snuggled against each other in Hunter's bed. My stomach rolls and I want to be sick. I scramble backwards until I bump into something behind me.

"You ready to howl, baby?" I hear Wolf say behind me.

Hands grip my arms and yank me up until I'm standing. My arms are pulled back and a hand wraps around my throat while the figure in front of me steps closer. His face is covered by the hood of the black sweaters they all had on before the game began. When he's close enough for the light of the moon to highlight his features, his blue-green eyes look black in the dark. I don't recognize the Hunter I've come to know over the last month in them anymore.

"Please, Hunter. Please don't," I beg, tears now streaking down my cheeks. He continues advancing on me while two of the other guys hold me still from behind.

"I'm sorry, Little Lamb," Kane whispers close to my ear, his lips brushing against the shell with each word.

"Noooo!"

The last lingering flock of birds takes off from high tree branches. Their squawks echoing in the otherwise silent night, and then… nothing.

Redeemed

Reminder of powers:
Hunter = Death
Kane = War
Wolf = Famine
Jagger = Plague

Andréa Joy

CHAPTER ONE

ARLO

December...

"DID YOU GET enough to eat, hunny?" Mom asks, standing from her seat across from me at the dining room table and reaching out to gather the serving bowl with left over Caesar salad.

"Plenty. Thank you," I reply, wiping the corners of my mouth with the red paper napkin beside my plate.

As soon as she turns her back and heads toward the kitchen, I let out the breath I've been holding all through dinner. Ever since she got the call saying that I was in the hospital with what was bordering on starvation and hypothermia, she's been hovering over me like a mother hen. I mean, I can't exactly blame her. I would be freaked out too if I got a call in the middle of the night saying that my only children was in hospital and the doctors weren't sure if they'd make it.

I can still see that night as clear as day in my mind whenever I close my eyes. Pain lances through my heart at the memory that the four men I was falling in love with had almost killed me. I was so stupid and naive. Why the hell would guys like that have any interest in someone like me?

I opted to finish out the rest of the semester online and Mom insisted that I move back in with her at least until the next semester starts. I didn't even need to think about it. I jumped at the opportunity to get out of Toronto and away from the four men who were responsible for putting me in the hospital. But as the winter break slowly winds down I'm not even sure if Queen's University is where I want to be. Can I handle running into any of them by chance? I'm not sure I can.

"You okay?"

I startle when Mom appears beside my chair, her one arm outstretched towards my plate.

"Yeah. Yeah, I'm good. Just a little tired I guess," I add with a shrug, and then push out my chair so that I can help her gather the rest of the dishes from the dinner table. "Is Adrian still coming over for dessert?"

Adrian is the guy Mom first went out on a date with in September. Things seem to be going well for them. He's a single parent too, but his son is a few years older than me. I found it odd that she didn't just invite both of them to spend Christmas with us seeing as how Adrian was having dinner with his son before coming over here. But I wasn't going to question it. Whatever worked for them was fine.

"He'll be here in a few minutes," Mom says, leading the way to the kitchen.

I help her rinse the dishes and load the dishwasher, but when Adrian still isn't here, I head to the living room to catch up on social media while Mom puts the finishing touches on the dessert she made. In previous years I would help her, but it quickly became apparent that baking is not my thing. I'd hate to ruin the hard work she put into it, so I just stay out of her way now. Pulling my phone from the back pocket of my black jeans, I collapse into an arm chair and kick my legs over one of the arms while I respond to several Christmas wishes on my timeline.

A post about half way down makes me pause in my scrolling. One of my favourites divers just posted an open invitation for people to join him in his next dive at Guadalupe Island. That's like the creme de la creme of shark dives. My thumb hits the link posted before my brain has a chance to catch up and my eyes greedily take in all the information about the trip. Until I get to the dates and my heart sinks.

July 2021.

I've already decided to do summer school this year so that I can potentially graduate a year early. But now… well, now I'm rethinking summer school. Guadalupe Island may never come around again. *The chance to dive with one of the men responsible for my love of Sharks may never come around again.*

I don't have time to debate the pros and cons of skipping summer school this year to go diving as the doorbell rings signalling Adrian's arrival for dessert.

The rest of the night goes off without a hitch. Adrian seems like a good man and he makes mom happy. I can't remember a time after dad died when I saw her this happy. When they start cuddling on the longer couch and sneaking kisses when they think I'm not looking, I decide to take that as my cue and wish them both a good-night before heading upstairs to my room.

Not bothering with a shower since I didn't go anywhere and didn't bother putting makeup on earlier, I shimmy out of my skinny black jeans and shuck off my top and bra and leave them on the floor to be picked up later. I grab a random worn out t-shirt from the top drawer of my dresser and pull it on then climb into bed, pulling the heavy duvet around me until I've made my own little cocoon.

It's not until I'm surrounded by cherry blossoms that the lingering scent on the t-shirt I just threw on registers. Warm vanilla musk and something else. Kane. My chest tightens and a sob threatens to break free but I swallow it down. I won't spend any more tears on those four. They don't deserve it.

My phone pings and I slip it out from under my pillow. My stomach drops when

I see that it's a text from Jules with an attachment. My thumb hovers over the text banner. One half of myself warring with the other half on whether I should open it or just swipe left and ignore it. Better yet, delete it. I haven't talked to Jules since Halloween. I felt guilty that her brother hadn't invited her to whatever party they were throwing at the cabin so I went to her haunted house thing first and then made up some lame excuse that I had to leave right after.

A part of me wonders if she knew what was going to happen that night, but that's not the Julie I've come to know. I thought the same thing about the guys, though, and my initial impression of them was severely wrong. I thought they felt something for me. That their actions proved I wasn't the only one who was falling in love. Which is what made what happened on Halloween night hurt even more.

I couldn't bear to see Julie, knowing that Kane was her stepbrother. I wanted nothing to do with Kane, Hunter, Wolf, and

Jagger. Unfortunately, that means having to distance myself from the only friend I have back at school. After staring at the screen until the banner almost seemed to mock me, I click the side button and push the phone back under my pillow choosing to ignore it after all.

Sleep doesn't come. Again. It's been almost two months since the last I had a decent night's sleep. Every time I close my eyes, those woods haunt me. The image of Hunter advancing on me like I was the prey he had finally caught in his cross-hairs, plagues me over and over again. No matter how hard I try, I can't shake that image nor the feel of hands holding me in place. I can still smell Wolf and Kane as they held me. As they made me watch my death get closer and closer. I can still feel Kane's lips against the shell of my ear as he whispered his last words to me.

"I'm sorry, Little Lamb."

He was sorry! He. Was. Sorry!?

My brain screams at me. How can he possibly be sorry for something he allowed to happen. At any time he could've stopped it, but he didn't. He allowed Hunter to do whatever it is he did to me. He *held* me back for fucks sake. So then why… why is it that every time I think of him, my brain conjures up the way his eyes almost disappear when he smiles, or how the green overpowers the gold when he's up to something.

I roll onto my back and pound the bed at my side with my fist a couple times. I wonder if it's too late to try and transfer schools for the upcoming semester. I heard Ryerson is supposed to be another good school. A knot forms in my gut and nausea rolls through me at the thought of never seeing either one of them again despite what they did to me in those woods.

As if it has a mind of its own, my hand slides under the pillow, searching for the phone I shoved under there a few short hours ago. The screen wakes up as soon as I pull it out from its dark cavern. The text message badge still stares up at me, begging me to read it. Running on very little sleep these past several weeks, I'm weak. I lift the phone to my face. My body burns with uncertainty as to what I'll find in the message when the locked icon at the top switches to unlocked. My stomach rolls and I roll with it until I'm lying on my side and kick the covers off in case I need to make a hasty get away to the bathroom. I click on Julie's message at the top and like a sucker punch, my breath leaves me in a whoosh.

Wish you were here is written in the caption.

Julie stands in the middle of the picture. Her hair, now a pastel blue, makes her natural blue eyes look paler, almost luminescent. And the black dress she's wearing just accentuates how beautiful she is. But it's not her my eyes are drawn too. It's the four guys surrounding her on either side. Their smiles are blinding, like they don't have a care in the world or they didn't just try and kill someone weeks ago and almost succeed. I'm almost certain that if a group of hikers hadn't found me when they did, I would've died out there. In fact, I did. According to the doctor at the hospital, my heart had stopped beating in the ambulance. My body temperature had dropped so low that they had a hard time getting it back up enough to where my heart wouldn't quit again. Still, that doesn't stop my thumb from tracing over Kane. Out of the four of them, his betrayal hurt the most.

Andréa Joy

CHAPTER TWO

ARLO

"YOU DON'T HAVE to go back there if you're not ready," Mom says, fluttering around the kitchen.

I didn't tell her the truth about what happened that night, but I think she has an idea. I definitely wasn't hiding my uncertainty of returning to Queen's this week, but mom's always have a way of knowing something without their kids having to tell them. It's eerie.

"I know," I say, picking up an apple from the fruit bowl on the counter and taking a bit. The juices run down the corners of my mouth and I have to catch it with my sleeve before it drips onto the front of my shirt.

Mom sighs, grabbing the dishtowel from where it's folded over the handle of the oven and dries her hands. "There are other schools that are just as good as Queen's University." Her dark brown eyes lock on mine and once again I'm shocked at their intensity. I have my dad's grey eyes, and as much as people would – and still do – ooh and aah over them, I used to wish that I had my mom's dark brown gaze. The brown doesn't give anything away as to what she's feeling or thinking. I love the mystery of that. She doesn't give me a chance to respond before she goes on. "You and your dad both are so drawn to that school and I'll never understand why." She refold the dishtowel over the oven handle and then grabs a knife from the block to chop the green peppers she placed on the cutting board earlier.

"Wait, dad wanted to go to Queen's too?"

Mom nods, peeling off the sticker on one of the peppers before reaching for the knife again. "For as long as I knew him, he couldn't stop talking about that school. He wanted both of us to attend." A sad smile graces her lips before it's gone and she frowns. "Said we were going to get a place off campus. No roommates, just us. He even talked about how he was going to get a job as a bartender at one of the pubs close by after he turned nineteen. He was so excited to live in the big city."

"What happened?" I ask, but as soon as the words leave my lips, I know. Me. I happened.

Mom smiles, putting down the knife and wiping her hands on the apron around her neck before stepping up to me and taking my face in her hands. "We got the greatest gift we never knew we wanted."

I grip her wrists in my hands. "It sounds like you didn't get your dreams, though." My heart plummets. If it weren't for me, my dad never would've had to join the Navy. Maybe he would've still been alive today. Maybe him and mom would've had the life they wanted.

She pulls me into her arms and kisses the top of my head. "Maybe we didn't get that dream, but the one we wanted the most became a reality. Don't ever doubt that you were wanted, Charlotte. Your father and I were so happy when we found out that we were having you. We might've been young by society standards, but love… *life* doesn't adhere to a timeline. It doesn't wait until the perfect time or when you think you're ready. That's what makes it an adventure. I thank God every day that he blessed us with you." She squeezes me to her and then pulls away only far enough so she can see my face. "Okay?"

Somehow, I manage to smile through the tears running down my face. "Okay."

"Good." She grins and I know what's coming next. "Now, will you tell me what really happened that night?"

"Mom," I groan, stepping away and forcing her to drop of her hands from my arms. She watches me walk over to the garbage and throwing out my apple core, but doesn't say anything. When I'm done I wash my hands in the sink and dry them before turning back to her. "I'm still not ready to talk about it, but when I am I promise I'll tell you."

She eyes me like she's not totally convinced I will and I have to fight against squirming under that eyebrow raise. Finally, she relents and goes back to chopping vegetables for my last dinner at home before going back to campus tomorrow.

"Alright. I'll let it go."

"Thank you." I kiss her cheek and then head upstairs to shower. I was able to drop in at one of the gyms in town while I've been home for the holidays. It feels good to be moving my body again. I was ordered to take it easy for a while after being released from hospital. Which was great for like the first week because it allowed me to catch up on shows on Netflix and books that I've had on my to-read list. But around week two, I started getting antsy. I'm pretty sure I drove mom bat shit crazy that week too, with my pacing around the house and constant need to keep moving. I didn't tell her that part of my need to keep moving was fear that if I stopped, I would relive that night. It was bad enough that at night when the house was quiet and I couldn't pace up and down, my brain would play those final seconds on a constant loop. Except, in the version in my head I never wake up. And I'm never found.

I'm just packing my hairdryer and other hair tools in my bag when the doorbell rings.

"I'll get it," I say, racing downstairs, knowing that mom is finishing off the little touches on dinner. "Hey, Adrian." I pull the door open wider and invite mom's boyfriend inside. She'd mentioned earlier in the week that she wanted me to meet Adrian's son before I went back to school. Apparently he goes to Queen's as well.

"Hi, Charlotte," Adrian greets, pulling me into one of his weird side hugs. "This is my son, Hunter."

I freeze at the name. My spine goes stiff and my fingers tighten around the door knob I'm still holding when I get a good look at the person stepping through the front door behind Adrian. No. Oh, no. No. No. No! This cannot be happening right now. Hunter stares back at me with a similar look of shock on his handsome face. Well, at least I'm not the only one taken aback by this realization. He's quicker to recover than I am, though, and sticks his hand out.

"Nice to meet you, Charlotte."

So, this is how we're playing it? Okay then. I grit my back teeth and slide my palm against his to shake his hand. Ignoring the way heat pools in my belly from just his touch. "You too." The *Asshole* is implied.

Hunter has the decency to look ashamed. He drops his gaze and takes his hand back, only to rake it through his dark hair. It's grown out a lot since the last time I saw him. Completely hanging in his face now and covering one eye. Thankfully, he doesn't linger and follows Adrian further into the house towards the kitchen where mom is plating dinner on the new serving dishes she got for Christmas. I close the door behind them and slump back against the painted wood.

"Dead God, give me strength," I whisper under my breath before pushing up off the door and joining everyone in the dining room.

I make my way back down the carpeted hallway to the dining room, pausing just outside the doorway. Mom's house doesn't have an open floor plan like the majority of newer houses do, and right now in this moment, I'm extremely grateful. The closed off room allows me the few breaths I need to mentally compose myself for eating dinner with Hunter. I still can't believe he's here in my house, and his father is dating my mother.

"So, Hunter, your dad tells me that you're student body president," Mom says, after we're all seated around the table and have filled our plates with the roast dinner she made.

Hunter shifts beside me, just a subtle rock from side to side but it's enough for his thigh to brush against mine. I still, part shock and part disappoint grips my heart at the heat that still flames to life at his touch.

"Yes, ma'am. Three years running," he answers, but his eyes are firmly locked onto his dad. A look passes between them that I can't desipher. Mom doesn't seem to notice as she cuts through a piece of roast and sweet potato.

"And you go to Queen's too?"

"Mom," I groan. "What's with the twenty questions?"

"What? I'm just trying to get to know him, Arlo," she says looking taken aback by my protest, but I see the glimmer in her eye. She's hoping that if she asks enough questions, it'll make me want to engage in conversation with Hunter. If only she knew…

"It's okay," Hunter says, breaking the stare down with his dad. "I don't mind."

Mom grins triumphantly and goes back to asking him a hundred-and-one questions. Hunter takes it in all in stride, answering each of them with just the right amount of charm to win her over while Adrian sits back quietly and observes the back and forth, only jumping in here and there.

By the time dessert is done and the table is cleared, my entire body aches from sitting so still. Every time I or Hunter would move, his thigh or his arm would brush against mine, fanning the flame that ignited at the beginning of dinner.

As soon as the dishes are loaded in the dishwasher, I excuse myself and race up the stairs to the solidarity of my room. I push open the door and swing it shut before falling back on my bed.

"Well, this was a nice surprise."

I bolt upright at the deep voice. My fingers curl into the duvet on either side of my thighs as I lock eyes with the man leaning against the door jam of my room. How did I not hear the door open?

"What are you doing up here? Better yet, what are you doing in my house?"

Hunter sighs, uncrossing his ankles and straightening up off the wall. "I didn't know she was your mom." We both look over his shoulder when mom giggles from somewhere downstairs. Hunter eases himself further inside my room and silently shuts the door behind him. "Look, you can't trust Adrian. He's not the guy you or your mom think he is."

"Oh? And who is he? Why should I even trust you, Hunter? After what you did to me."

He opens and closes his mouth but no sounds come out. Finally, he steps forward. Pain flashes behind his eyes but then he blinks and its gone. It doesn't matter anyway.

"You shouldn't," he says, finally, shocking me. "What we did is unforgivable, but we did it to try and protect you." He looks over his shoulder toward the door. When he looks back he drops his chin to his chest. "I can see now that it was stupid." He lifts his head back up to look at me and reaches out a hand but drops it before he can touch me. "Please, just don't trust Adrian."

He turns to leave but I can't let me go without asking, "isn't he your dad? Why are you warning me against him?"

Hunter pauses with his hand on the door handle, his back still to me. "He's not my father," he says, and then pulls open the door and disappears. A few minutes later I hear the beep of the alarm as the front door is opened and closed.

CHAPTER THREE

HUNTER

"YOU SAW HER?" Kane asks, jumping up from his wingback chair beside Jagger.

"I did." My finger taps out a rhythm I have a hard time following in my head. I'm too distracted. Too focused on the fear I saw in Arlo's eyes when we were alone in her bedroom. I never thought seeing her afraid of me would gut me as much as it did, but it nearly destroyed me. We did that. We took our sweet, Little Lamb, and made her afraid to be in the same room as one of us. I curse and push up out of my own chair. My hands shake as I reach for the glass decanter on the bar cart in the corner of the room.

"That's it?" Jagger says. "That's all you're going to say."

They're standing behind me now. All three of them with their arms crossed over their chest. The glow from the fireplace dancing across their features, making them even more handsome than any of them have any right to be.

"She was scared of being alone with me." The ice in the glass clink together as I bring the drink to my lips. The spicy flavour of the liquor burns the back of my throat on the way down.

Silence descends upon the room like a dark cloud. The weight of my words registering with the three of them.

"Well, did you try to explain?"

My fingers tighten around the glass until my knuckle turn white with the force. "And what would you have me say?" I spit, spinning on Kane and getting in his face. I know it'll be a long time before I'm able to forget the look on Arlo's face when I close my eyes at night. "They knew! All this time and they've fucking known!" I turn and begin pacing the length of the room. "Randall has instigated himself in her mother's life for fucks sake! It doesn't matter what we try to tell her, they'll know."

I stop in front of one of the built-in bookshelves and lean my palms against it, letting my head fall forward. Things were supposed to be easier after that night. With Arlo seemingly out of the picture, The Elders were supposed to go back to doing whatever they do the rest of the year. We didn't expect them to stay in Canada. To be so close. We thought that by now we would've gotten to explain everything to her. We had plans on sweeping her away to a cabin up north for Christmas. Just the five of us. But with The Elders sticking

around, it made it impossible. And now…
well, now it could be too late.

"Fuck!" I roar, my hands moving to
sweep everything off the shelves before my
brain has a chance to catch up. I don't stop
until hundreds of books and collectibles
are littering the floor around me.

The guys stand behind me, just
watching. Each of them lost in their own
thoughts.

"We have to tell her," Wolf says, his
voice so low that it's almost a whisper in
the room.

"She won't be believe us," I say, my
shoulders slumping forward in defeat.

"We still have to try," Kane adds while
Jagger nods his agreement.

"She already hates us so what's the
worst that could happen?" Wolf shrugs.

"They could kill her."

Jagger moves to pick up some of the
fallen books from the floor. "They could
kill her now. They must at least suspect that
she has something to do with breaking the
curse. She's more vulnerable without us."

I don't argue with him because he's right. For a while now I've suspected that they've just been abiding their time. Trying to figure out exactly what role she plays in reversing the curse they conjured a century ago. At least we know that they have no idea that three of us have slowly been getting our gifts back because if they did, Arlo would've been dead already. Wolf and Kane begin picking up books too and restocking them on their respective shelves.

"She at least has a chance with us protecting her. Especially with three of us gaining our powers back." This from Kane.

One by one they stop and turn their attention on me. I sigh, pinching the bridge of my nose between my thumb and forefinger. "The semester starts on Monday. From the looks of it, she's planning on heading back to campus either tonight or tomorrow morning. One of us should be there to try and talk to her."

"Me. I'll do it," Kane says, but I'm already shaking my head.

"No. Jagger or Wolf should be the ones to go." At Kane's crestfallen look, I pull him into my arms and press a kiss to the top of his head. "You two were the closets. She probably feels hurt by you the most."

Kane whines low in his throat and I tighten my hold around his shoulders. Kane has always been the one in our group who feels the hardest. He fell fast and hard for our girl, and I don't blame him. She's one hell of a girl. I pull away just enough to see his face. Cupping his cheek in one hand I lean down and kiss him.

The kiss starts out slow at first. Just a press of lips, and then his tongue peeks out to lick between the seam of my lips and I open for him, wedging a knee between his legs as I do. Kane groans and curls a hand around the nap of my neck, pulling me closer to him so he can deepen the kiss. It takes all my strength to not take control of the kiss. Of him. But this is what he needs and I'll gladly give it to him.

It doesn't take long before he's humping my thigh, seeking the friction he craves. Somewhere in the back of my mind I register the same sounds coming from Wolf and Jagger, but I'm too lost in Kane's kiss to look. I back him up until the back of his legs hit the solid wood desk. I grip his hips in my hands and spin him around. His hands shoot out to brace against the surface with the momentum.

"Don't move your hands," I say, nipping at his neck and grinding my aching cock against his ass.

Kane moans, arching his back and pushing his bubble butt further into me.

Jagger moves around the front of the desk and steps out of his pants before climbing on top and shuffling on his knees until his crotch is right in front of Kane's face. His fist moves languidly up and down his length until a bead of pre-cum pearls at the head of cock. Then he paints Kane's lips with the salty liquid. I fist Kane's hair and pull his head back, forcing his back to arch more, and growl a reminder into his ear as Wolf's hands begin to roam my torso.

"Do not remove those hands from the desk, Kane."

His only response is a long groan as Jagger pushes his cock between Kane's lips. Wolf's hard chest presses into my back, his lips kissing a path up my neck as his hands slowly lift the shirt up and off my body.

"You going to let me fuck you this time?" He asks, trailing a finger between the waistband of my jeans and my skin.

I chuckle. "That depends," I say, reaching around Kane to undo his belt and push his pants and underwear to the floor. The move forces me to bend over and Wolf groans behind me, grabbing my hips in his hands and thrust his pelvis forward. A shiver races up my spine. "Have you earned it?"

"I've been a very good boy," Wolf says, sliding a hand over my crotch, under my jeans.

An idea pops into my head and my dick twitches at the thought. We've never done it before, but I'm suddenly very eager to give it a try. I run my hands down Kane's back, feeling goosebumps pebble his skin as I go until I'm bent back over. My face within inches of his ass and my ass press into the front of Wolf's pants where there's a very big bulge.

"Get me ready then," I say over my shoulder and then smirk when Wolf's eyes darken with lust.

Turning back to Kane, I palm his cheeks open and lick a stripe up from his balls to his crack. He shivers and then groans, pushing back into my face.

"Oh fuck," Jagger, groans, dropping his head back onto his shoulder and fucking Kane's mouth faster.

"Don't fucking come yet, Jagger. Not until we're both filling up his tight hole."

Kane stiffens under my hands and then the sweetest whimper leaves his throat. I continue my ministrations on his hole and only add a finger when he's nice and wet. Kane moans, pushing back on my finger as I work it in and out. I hear the snick of a bottle cap being closed before a bottle of lube appears beside my head and cold, wet fingers circle my hole. I take the bottle from Wolf and groan, straightening up a little when his finger pushes forward passed the tight ring of muscle.

Wolf's breath hitches. A warm palm lands on my back and pushes me back down. "Fuck. You're so damn tight, H."

"Oh, fuck. Fuck fuck fuck," Kane pants, getting Jagger cock fall from his lips when I add another finger. "Please," he begs, drawing out the word.

I remove my fingers from Kane's hole and Wolf takes a step back allowing me to straighten to my full height. Jagger scrambles off the desk and goes to lie down on the carpet in front of the fireplace. Kane follows after him and straddles his waist. Wolf and I stand in a trance, watching Kane take Jagger's full length. Both of our cocks hard and pointing at the scene in front of us.

Jagger laughs and then groans when Kane starts rocking back and forth. "You two just gonna watch or you planning on joining?"

That's enough to get my feet moving. I take up position behind Kane and press a palm to his back, encouraging him to lean forward. Jagger grips Kane's hips and keeps him still while I push inside beside Jagger's cock. Kane whims and Jagger runs soothing hands up and down his back while whispering into his ear. Too low for Wolf or I to hear. Whatever he's saying is enough to get Kane relax and I slide the rest of the way inside.

"Fucking hell," I say between clenched teeth. Kane's hole was already fucking tight but with both Jagger and I inside, it's incredible.

I stay still, giving Kane some time to adjust to having two cocks in his ass. When he relaxes a bit more, I give a few experimental thrusts that have both him and Jagger moaning. After a while, I feel Wolf moving up to squat behind me and cold liquid drizzles down my hole. When I feel the head of Wolf's cock against my hole, I grip Kane's neck and force him to look over his shoulder so I can kiss him. He swallows my groan of pain like it's favourite candy and soon I'm panting. With my cock enveloped by a tight heat and Wolf's cock pegging my prostate, I'm not going to last long. And by the sounds of it, neither are the others.

"Are you going to come for us, Kane? Going to paint Jagger's stomach with your seed?" I nip and suck a trail up his shoulder and neck to below his ear.

It doesn't matter what shit is going on in our lives or how far we fall away from each other, this right here always has the ability to bring everything back down. Knowing that these three wills always be there to catch me is enough for me to believe that whatever happens or doesn't happen with Arlo, it'll be okay. She may be the missing piece of the puzzle that completes us, but if it turns out that she can't or won't forgive us then we'll find a way to carry on without her... together.

"Shit," Jagger says, intertwining his fingers with mine on Kane's hips. He thrusts up causing his length to slide against mine inside of Kane, and my eyes roll back. The tip of his cocks rubbing against the underside of mine. Fuck that feels good.

Wolf's thrusts speed up, the momentum pushing me into Kane faster. Kane shudders and drops his head to Jagger's shoulder as his hole tightens with his release. Jagger plants his feet firmly on the carpet beside my knees and arches up, forcing his cock further in alongside mine and then hot spurts of cum fill Kane around my cock which triggers my own release. I grunt, fucking more of my cum inside Kane. Wolf grunts, clamping a hand on my shoulder and pulling me back to meet each on of his hard thrusts. I'm covered so covered in sweat that he can't get a good grip. Eventually, he curses and drops down to his knees, pulling me up against him so my back is plastered to his chest. I reach around him and grab onto his thigh, the muscle pulling and contracting under my hand.

I'm still inside Kane so every hard thrust forward of Wolf's hips, sends my cock further into Kane's sensitive hole and against Jagger's still semi-hard dick. Both of them groan.

"Can't wait til I can hold you down and fuck you like I really want to," Wolf pants in my ear, his arm tightening around my chest like a band.

"Yes," I breathe. My dick hardens to full mast again and I feel like I can come a second time. "Wolf. Argh, fuck!"

He bites down on my neck, his teeth sinking into the flesh of the curve and then he's filling me up so good I can feel it leaking out and running down the inside of my thighs. My legs are like jell-o, I collapse on top of Kane's back, barely having a thought to brace my arms on either side of Jagger's head before I squash them both.

"Holy fuck," Kane breathes as we're all trying to catch our breath.

"My thoughts exactly," I say, nuzzling the side of Kane's neck.

"As much as I'm loving this cuddle pile. We're all sweaty and sticky, and I have major rug burn on my back. Can we maybe move this to the shower? Or the bed?"

I chuckle and then groan when I pull out of Kane. Wolf offers me a hand up and then together we help Kane and Jagger up from the floor. Jagger yelps when Wolf smacks his ass, leaving a nice red hand print on his ass cheek, as he walks by.

"You'll pay for that," Jagger growls when Wolf shoulders passed him and out into the hallway.

"I'd like to see you try," Wolf volleys back.

Andréa Joy

CHAPTER FOUR

ARLO

QUEEN'S UNIVERSITY.

I can't believe it's been four months since the first time I stood right here and looked up at the imposing structure. A giddy excitement coupled with nervousness thrum through my veins. A lifetime of dreams had accumulated to that point. It had felt like I was home.

Now, as I stare up at the same building cold dread curls around my stomach in a fist and squeezes. *What am I doing here?* Flashes of a memory from not long ago causes me to stumble against the brick building. With my back against the wall, I bend over bracing my palms on my knees, trying in vain to stop the dry heaving that seems to come naturally now every time I think about Halloween night.

"I can't do this," I say to no one in particular as I straighten off the wall.

Not that anyone walking passed cares about my issues. I turn around, settling on the decision to walk back to my apartment and put in for a transfer in the morning, but then a group of students turning down the side of the building catches my attention. I follow a few paces behind. Eventually a path between the buildings comes into view. Last semester I was pretty rigid in my routine while on campus. I entered and left through the main building. The only time I left through the parking lot at the opposite end of campus was when I stayed after class and waited for Jagger to be done with football practise. I knew there were random paths that weaved around and between buildings that lead to different places, but I never followed them. My sense of direction is almost non-existent. It was easier for me to find a way that worked and didn't get me lost and stick to it.

I follow the group of students down the path and out the other side. It takes me a lot longer than I'd like to catch my bearings but eventually I find my way to my first class of the day. Unlike last semester, I have classes every day except for Friday's with Thursday's being my longest day. My last class on Thursday gets out at 9 p.m. Just like last semester, I find a seat at the back of the lecture hall and take out my laptop while I wait for the class to start. I'm catching up on my favourite Instagram account on my phone when someone sits in the seat beside. They lean so far over that their elbow is now resting on my arm rest. I go to tell them to move but when I get a good look at who it is, I freeze. My mouth gapes and I'm pretty sure I look like a fish with the way I'm opening and closing it.

"The Galápagos, huh?" Wolf whistles low, leaning in closer to get a better look at my phone. "I've been there. Lots of fish. Not the greatest vacation spot, though."

"What are you doing here?" I hiss, shoving my phone back in my purse and looking around the room.

"All the seats are taken, Little Lamb. There's nowhere to run." The bastard has a smug smile on his face when he sees the panicked look on my face.

"Don't call me that!" I start gathering my stuff and I'm about to put my laptop back in its case when the Prof begins the lecture. I chew on the corner of my lip, wondering if I can sneak down the side without every eye watching me. I glance behind me, but there aren't any doors up here.

Wolf chuckles, leaning back in his seat and giving me more room. He kicks his feet out in front of him looking every bit unaffected. "Relax, Little Lamb. It's only an hour and twenty minutes."

I glance at the door at the bottom of the stairs again and then scan the room filled with students and not an empty seat in sight. I sigh, opening my laptop again and try to ignore the asshole sitting beside me. But when half an hour goes by and my page is still blank because I'm so hyper-focused on every move and every sound Wolf makes that I haven't heard a word the Prof has said, I give up and settle back in my seat with my arms crossed.

"I'm sorry."

I startle, not expecting those words to come from him.

"Excuse me?" A couple of the girls sitting in the row in front of us turn to glare. "Sorry," I mouth to them. When they turn back toward the front of the room, I turn to Wolf. "You're sorry!?"

"*We're* sorry," he whispers, leaning over and closing the gap between our seats.

I snort, turning to face the front again and make a mental note to check if there's another section for this class. Even if there isn't I'll just drop it and take another English class to satisfy the requirement or try again next year. Surely they'll be graduated by then.

"Little Lamb." Wolf's hand comes to land on my arm and I jerk it away. He sighs but doesn't move to touch me again. "Arlo, please just let us explain."

"Explain," I shriek, but thankfully everyone has stood up and are packing their things. "Explain what exactly? Why you tried to kill me?"

Wolf quickly glances around the room but nobody's paying us any attention and the room is beginning to empty out. "We can't do this here. Look, just come to the house tonight. We'll make dinner." His dark brown eyes plead with me to accept, but I can't.

"Go fuck yourself, Wolf." I gather my things and race down the stairs and out the door.

Jagger, Kane, and Hunter are standing by the vending machine down the hall right next to the exit. They all look over at me simultaneously. Hunter's brows draw down in the middle while Jagger looks me up and down in a slow perusal. But it's Kane's eyes that almost kill me. Sadness pools in the whiskey depths. He tries to take a step forward when he sees me but Hunter holds him back.

"Arlo," Wolf says from behind me. "Please," he pleads, but I'm already shaking my head.

I turn and run down the hallway away from the four of them. I don't stop until I'm pulling the door open to my apartment building. It's not until I get inside my apartment and close the door to my room that I realize I'm crying. My heart feels like it's physically breaking inside my chest. I want to scream and throw things. I want to march up to them and demand to know why they did what they did. I want… I sigh and flop down on my back on the mattress. I wanted to walk up to them and kiss them all. To feel their arms around me again.

How is it that they attacked me. Almost succeeded in killing me, and yet all I can think of is being with them again. Of things going back to the way they were before Halloween.

"Arlo, please let us explain."

Wolf's eyes looked so haunted when he pleaded with me to hear them out. Actually, all the guys looked like they hadn't slept more than a couple hours in the months that have passed. I should feel elated at that, shouldn't I? And Kane… tears pool in my eyes as I roll onto my side and tug my hands under my cheek. He looked heartbroken when Hunter held him back from coming to me.

So, maybe I do go hear them out? What then? No explanation they give me could possibly eradicate what they did.

But what if it does? Are you willing to walk away from them completely? Are you willing to forget you ever heard their names?

Am I?

I pull out my phone from my pocket and search through the messages until I find the photo Jules sent me on Christmas evening. Why do I get the feeling that walking away from the four of them will be the gravest mistake I ever make?

Andréa Joy

CHAPTER FIVE

KANE

"**S**HE'S NOT GOING to come," I say, pacing back and forth in front of the guys. My entire body is vibrating and I feel like at any moment I could vibrate out of my skin. Even the cold permeating the air around us can't touch me right now. I'm hyper-focused on the fact that Arlo even agreed to see us after Jagger texted her a few days after we saw her in the hallway at school.

I couldn't take the hurt look on her face when she turned and saw the three of us standing there. I wanted to go to her, drop down on my knees, and beg for her forgiveness. I would do anything to get back the Arlo from before that night in the woods. The same woods that surround us on three sides. Maybe this wasn't the greatest place to do this, but it's the only place where we can show her everything in relative privacy. Relative because we never know if The Elders have sent someone else to watch us or if they're slinking around here somewhere. I wouldn't put it past them, but it's a risk we have to take.

"She'll come," Hunter says, sounding so sure of himself.

My hands curl into fists at my side and I have to hold myself back from punching him. This is his damn fault. If he hadn't spewed that shit about her not meaning anything to us then we wouldn't have been forced to do what we did.

But what if he hadn't?

I stop my pacing and stare straight ahead through a small opening in the trees but not seeing them. My mind back to the day when they found out we hadn't succeeded in killing her.

"We meant to ask you, when's the funeral?" James asks, tapping his fingers against the glass of bourbon in his hand.

"Who's funeral?" Jagger tilts his head in feigned confusion. To anyone else the look would seem genuine, but the four of us know what James is really fishing for.

"The girl," Sean interjects, his nose flaring in frustration.

Hunter sits back in his seat, the meal in front of him forgotten, as he stares James down. My eyes flicker across to Randall whose face is a stoneless mask. Dread sits like a concrete weight in my gut. They know.

"Tell me," Hunter starts. I swallow hard and make eye contact with Jagger and Wolf. To the outside world, they look clam, relaxed. But I see the same unease

*swimming in their eyes. Hunter contin-
ues, "why do you think we'd go to her
funeral? Or even care? We told you she
meant nothing."*

*Pride swells in my chest for Hunter.
His voice is calm, his tone deliberately
nonchalant and yet conveys just how
annoyed the question made him. He's act-
ing every bit the centuries old guardian he
once was. And will be again. Some called
us Angels, and we were for the most part,
but when we were sent down to Earth,
we were Guardians. Our job was to prevent Chaos from rising. Literally. He's not
someone you want to meet face to face.
The dude's scary. Scarier than Hades. We
failed on the guardian part and when The
Elders completed the curse, we lost our
wings and our gifts. It was only Hunter
bargaining with Hades to keep Chaos
leashed a bit longer that has saved humanity from diving into anarchy. However, that
time limit is almost up and if we don't do
something, and fast, we won't be able to
stop whatever happens next.*

James chuckles, but it's not humorous. "Do you think us fools?"

Silence descends around the room except for the creek of a door opening and closing nearby.

James stands from his spot at the head of the table. Sean and Randall stand from their seats as well. And one by one like grim reapers emerging from the shadows, four men step out from behind each of our chairs. I grip Hunter's leg under the table and he settles a warm hand over mine. A quiet reassurance that whatever happens, the four of us will be together.

"This might have turned out better for all of you if you'd just been honest with us about the girl," James says, resting the palms of his hands on the table beside his plate.

"You can't kill us," Wolf seethes, banging his fists on the opulent wood.

"No, I can't. You're right. But I can do something so heinous that you'll be wishing you could die once it's done." He gives a clipped nod to the men behind us *and suddenly we're yanked from our seats and marched down the winding, wooden staircase into a darkened room. I would say the lone swinging light is a bit cliché if it wasn't currently our reality.*

Wolf: You guys can practice using your gifts any time now.

Jagger: Is that wise? We don't want them to know that three of the four of us have access to them without their knowledge.

Hunter: Jagger is right. The longer we can put off them finding out, the better. It won't be hard for them to find out how we got our gifts back when they do find out.

Kane: If we even make it through this.

Wolf lays a reassuring hand on my shoulder but he's forced away before the contact can even register. The four of us are strapped into chairs that look like they belong in a dentist office of horrors. Fuck this is going to hurt. The thing that sucks about being immortal is that while we may not die, we still feel everything. Every snick of the blade as it cuts our skin, every jab of a needle, every bolt of electricity from a live wire. We feel it all.

"Hey, she'll be here," Jagger says, clamping a hand on my shoulder and drawing me out of the memories of those few weeks we spent in those chairs. If there was ever a Hell on Earth, it would be what we went through at the hands of James and the other Elders.

Now, with Randall having inserted himself into Arlo's life, we no longer feel the need to hide our connection to her. Being apart from her these last few months has been hard on all of us. Whatever had been concealing her from us for the last nineteen years disappeared the moment she stepped foot on the land Queen's University now resides on. A new bond forming in its place and that only strengthened the more time we spent with her.

Wolf sucks in a breath behind me causing me to spin around. The minute my eyes connect with the most beautiful grey eyes I've ever seen in my life, Wolf whispers, "Arlo."

My breath catches in my throat as I watch her standing there so unsure of us after what we did. Shame like I've never felt before courses through my veins, constricting my chest. The urge to drop to my knees at her feet even stronger now than it was the other day. What the fuck did we do? How could we do what we did to someone we love, and call it protection? Before I'm aware of what I'm doing, my feet carry me forward until I'm standing within inches of her. Arlo flinches back at my sudden proximity but doesn't move away. Her eyes widen as I slowly drop to my knees in the pristine, white snow and hang my head. The wind whips against my exposed skin as it picks up, but I don't care. My only focus is the woman standing above me.

"Kane, what are you doing?" Her voice is barely above a whisper, coated in hesitation and something else.

I sense someone move up beside me. A strong hand threads through my hair, sending shivers down my back, and then

Jagger drops to his knees on my left. Wolf is next on my right.

"What's going on? Why are you kneeling in the snow?" Arlo asks.

"There's a lot you don't know about us and where we came from," Hunter says, standing on Wolf's other side. "But we've only ever kneeled before one other being. This-"He pauses to sink down on his knees too. I noticed how he didn't say *person* but *being*. "Is our way of saying our lives belong to you now. Whatever it is you desire; we'll lay down our lives trying to make it true."

"What?" Arlo covers her mouth with a hand. Little lines appear at the corners of her eyes as she squints down at the four of us in confusion. "I-I don't understand."

She spins around, giving us her back, and my heart breaks even more if that's possible. The four of us continue to stay kneeling in the snow. Frost bite will just be another punishment heaped on us for what we did. But we'll take it freely. After a couple more minutes she turns back around.

Her arms folded across her chest as she takes us all in again.

"Get up, please, you must all be freezing. Where are your jackets?"

One by one we slowly rise to our feet, albeit somewhat reluctantly. I would've stayed kneeling until she forgave us, but she's right. The cold is starting to get to me. She looks at us expectantly when we haven't answered her question. Jagger stuffs his hands in the front pockets of his jeans and shrugs. His arms, red from the cold. I glance down at my own tattooed arms and notice they're the same almost cherry red colour from the wind.

"We asked you here to try and explain what happened and why," Hunter says.

Arlo pulls her bottom lip between her teeth and begins to chew on it as her eyes dart from us to the woods surrounding all of us and back again. Where there were once lush greenery decorating the branches, they're bare. But her unease about being in this place is still palpable.

I wish the location was different, but this is where it needs to happen.

"Ookay," she says, drawing out the word.

"It'll be easier to show you and then if you have any questions we'll answer them, alright?" Hunter says, and Arlo nods.

Wolf moves to stand beside Arlo in case anything goes wrong. Truth be told, we haven't tried what we're about to do. Hopefully it works. I suck in a deep breath and close my eyes. As I let out the breath, I concentrate on the rush of electricity down my arms and out my fingertips. When I open my eyes again, Arlo's eyes are wide, her skin pale. I glance to my right and see black lightning-bolt like sparks coming off Jagger. I look to my left and the same thing is happening with Hunter but his are a bright white, almost pale. Glancing down at my own hands, there are red sparks.

"Arlo!"

Jagger's sudden shout has my head snapping up in time to see Arlo's eyes rolling into the back of her skull as she sways

and begins to fall backward. Thankfully,
Wolf is there to catch her before her body
hits the ground.

CHAPTER SIX

"HOW IS SHE?" I ask, sliding off the bar stool as Hunter walks into the kitchen.

He moves around the room, getting a glass and pouring himself water from the jug in the fridge. He takes a drink, his Adam's apple bobbing with each swallow before he replies. "She's okay. Resting for now. Doctor said to just keep an eye on her."

As a unit, the four of us move to take seats around the dining room table. The mood in the room is somber as we all relive the moment Wolf barely had time to catch Arlo as she fainted. My heart has never raced as fast as it did when I saw her eyes roll back and her skin pale, not even when I told the guys I loved them just over a century ago.

"We can't tell her any more. She won't be able to handle it," I say, twirling my own glass of water in my hand.

"What choice do we have? She's in more danger now," Kane says, a scowl on his face.

"Jagger's right," Wolf adds, turning on the bench seat so his thighs are straddling me. "If she can't handle seeing the physical manifestation of your...our," he corrects when I stare him down. "Gifts then what's to say she can handle the rest of it? What's going to happen when we miss the deadline and Hades has to let Chaos go? Or Heaven forbid, the Elders decide to capture her." He shakes his head, a solemn look in his eyes. "I'm not about to put her through all that if it's going to cause her pain."

We're silent for a while. The hum of the furnace the only sound in the dimly lit cabin. Each of us lost in our own thoughts and memories no doubt.

"I think we're all underestimating her," Hunter says into the quiet room.

The three of us turn to look at him. Kane shuffles around on the other bench so that he can better see Hunter. Hunter's head is down, his gaze focused on the glass in his hands as his thumb wipes away the condensation.

"I think she'll surprise us. We just have to give her a chance. Plus, she has a right to know whether we think she's ready for it or not. It's part of her history too."

"But there's a reason Joseph didn't leave anything behind for her when he died. Do you think if he wanted his daughter to know he would've left her something? Some clue as to her heritage?" I argue.

Wolf lays a hand on my shoulder and tugs until I'm leaning back into him. He wraps his big arms around my waist and surrounds me in his comforting warmth. It's not that I don't want her to know everything. It would be such a relief to not have to keep secrets anymore, but we've already hurt her enough. I can't stand the thought of adding more hurt on top of it.

"What if he didn't have time?" Kane whispers, drawing our attention to him. He slowly lifts his head from watching his fingers toy with the hem of his sweater and locks eyes with each one of us. "We don't actually know what happened to him, but we're assuming he knew he was about to die."

We're silent again as Kane's words sink in. He's right. From the minute we found out about Arlo and who she was, we were operating under the assumption that her father, Joseph, knew he was going to do die and that's why he placed whatever protection he used over her, but what if that wasn't the case at all? I rub my forehead in hopes the headache beginning to take root, goes away. This is all too much information and a lot of unknowns.

"So what do we do now?" Wolf says, his chest rumbling against my back with each word, making my dick twitch. God, it's been awhile. I shift back, forcing him to spread his legs wider. Wolf's hand grip my hips and he groans low in his throat, nipping at my ear. "Behave yourself."

Kane clears his throat. Pink spreading across his cheeks as he watches us. A wicked smirk spreads across Hunter's face but it disappears as a more serious look takes its place.

"We tell her. All of it."

A creek of a floorboard sounds upstairs, gaining all of our attention. Kane sighs, leaning his head on Hunter's shoulder. "Everything's about to change."

"It already has," Hunter says, wrapping an arm around Kane's shoulders.

Gathering a plate and glass of orange juice, I take a tray upstairs to Arlo. She's sitting at the foot of the bed, her hands in her lap and that bottom lip pulled between her teeth again.

"I thought you might be hungry," I say, setting the tray on the dresser beside the door and sitting down beside her. "How are you feeling?"

She huffs out a laugh with a shake of her head. Soft, dark curls fall over her shoulder. "I should hate being back here," she says, looking around the room.

"But?"

Her gaze sweeps across the room to land back on me. Her smile is small, tentative. "But I don't. I should hate all of you, but I don't. I can't. And trust me, I've tried." Arlo pushes up from the bed and walks over to the window overlooking the backyard and the tree line of the forest ahead, pushing the curtains apart as she stares out. "I can't explain it, Jagger, but every time I think about walking away from all of you, I can't stomach it. It feels like my heart is being ripped into a million pieces. That's crazy, right? We haven't known each other that long."

I'm surprised she hasn't brought up what she saw earlier today in the field to the right of the property. I push off the bed and walk up behind her. Gently laying my hands on her shoulders. She stills for a moment but then relaxes under my touch.

"It's not crazy, Charlotte. We feel it too."

She shivers when I move her hair off her shoulder and lean down to press a kiss on her warm skin. "Was I dreaming? Did you really have sparks coming out of your fingertips?" Her voice is low, and if I wasn't leaning down close to her I wouldn't have heard it.

My entire body freezes as I reply, "You weren't dreaming."

She spins in my arms, her grey eyes ping pong between mine as her lips part. "I-I don't understand."

I cup her neck in my hands and rub my thumbs up and down along her jaw. "There's a lot we need to tell you. A lot of it isn't going to seem real, but I need you to keep an open mind, okay? I don't think it's a mistake that the five of us were brought together, but if you want nothing to do with us after you hear what we have to say then we'll find a way to leave you alone."

She sucks her bottom lip between her teeth again and I groan, dropping my forehead down to hers. From up close like this it looks like there are specks of blue and fiery red in her grey eyes. I suck in a breath at the familiarity of those colours.

"Jagger," she breathes, her lips within an inch of mine as her fingers curl around the shirt at my hips and pulls me closer.

Her eyes drop to my lips and I can't help closing the last bit of distance between us. My lips cover hers in a kiss that both pains and excites me. I drink down the taste of her on my tongue. I thought I would never get to taste her again. I resigned myself to the fact that I would never be able to kiss her or feel her body move under my hands again.

"Jesus," I groan, pulling back. We're both panting hard after that kiss. I brush her hair from her forehead with a finger and smile when she leans into my touch. "We should go downstairs."

"Okay."

She doesn't protest when I slip my hand into hers and pull her with me. I make a mental note to come back up later to grab the tray of food as we descend the stairs and walk into the living room where the other three guys are already waiting.

Wolf and Kane sit on the second love seat. Hunter sits on the leather recliner which leaves the longer couch for Arlo and me. I pull her down beside me and immediately breathe a silent sigh of relief when she presses into my side.

She rubs her palms down her jean clad thighs and then reaches over to grab my hand. I give her a reassuring squeeze and she smiles.

"I'm ready to listen," she says, turning back to face the other guys.

"Have you ever heard of the four horsemen?" Hunter asks, leaning forward to rest his elbows on his knees.

"You mean the nickname everyone at school calls you or from the seven seals?" She asks, confused. Probably wondering what the group in the Bible have to do with what happened in the woods on Halloween and in the field earlier today. "What does that have to do with what happened?" She asks after her first question is met with a round of nods.

"It's not just a Bible story, Charlotte," Hunter says, absently rubbing his hands together as he watches her reaction, as we all watch her.

"What do you mean it's not just a Bible story?"

I give her hand another squeeze and then twist so I can see her better. The move requires us to put more space between our bodies and I'm momentarily disappointed at the loss of heat from her body.

"Two centuries ago, we were sent to patrol the earth. Our main job was to make sure Chaos didn't reign on Earth," I say.

"We were supposed to keep order. Part of that was deciding who lived and who died through war, famine, and plague," Wolf adds.

"But," Kane joins in, "on our first night on Earth we were cursed by a group called The Elders."

"Our gifts were bound to them, but once they realized that they couldn't wield them without us, they altered the curse. Whenever they need someone dealt with, they allow us to gain our gifts back for those few hours. When the task is complete, they deplete us of them again."

"And that doesn't make you weak?" Arlo asks, looking to each of us.

I smile and my heart warms at the possibility that she might take this well after all. "It does, but after two centuries you kinda get used to it." I shrug it off, but it's really not as painless as I make it sound. For days afterward we're practically useless. We lack the energy to do even the simplest of tasks like brush our teeth or bathe.

"Why are you telling me all this?"

One by one all our eyes are drawn to Hunter since he's been the unspoken leader in all of us, after all he's the oldest by two months. Hunter clears his throat then swallows hard, looking at each of us in turn before directing his full attention to Arlo.

"None of us have been able to use our gifts without The Elders releasing them first, but," he pauses, leaning back in his seat. "But some of us began getting the ability to use our gifts independently of The Elders last semester. After we met you," he adds.

"Some of you?"

"Wolf hasn't gained the ability to access his yet."

"Wha-" Arlo trails off before she can finish her sentence.

Wolf rolls his eyes and sits forward. "What these idiots are trying to say is that we think you're the reason for the change. We think you… our relationship," he corrects before going on, "is the key to breaking the curse."

Arlo stares at him, mouth agape for several seconds before she clamps her jaw shut and leaves the rest of us in agonizing silence for what feels like years before she speaks again, but I wasn't expecting to hear what comes out of her mouth next.

"If you guys were sent to make sure chaos didn't reign, and you were cursed since that first night then… what or who has taken over that job."

Kane chuckles, earning a shoulder slap from Hunter who had gotten up to pace the living room at some point during Wolf's explanation.

"I made a deal with someone. It's being taken care of," Hunter says, wavering off the subject.

Kane sighs, slumping back in the love seat. "We can't keep lying to her, Hunter."

"It's not a lie! It's being handled."

"But not for long," Kane shouts, pushing to his feet and spinning on Hunter. His amusement from earlier gone. Their faces so close together that the tip of their noses are touching. "No more secrets," Kane whispers, gripping Hunter's neck and pressing their foreheads together.

Hunter grips Kane's hips. With his eyes squeezed shut he nods and presses a kiss to Kane's lips before pulling back. He looks over Kane's shoulder to Arlo, his eyes swimming with warring emotions.

"I made a deal with Hades to keep Chaos occupied for a couple centuries while we got everything figured out."

"Wait," Arlo says, jumping to her feet. "Chaos is an actual person?"

Wolf snorts and stands. I do too since everyone else is. "I wouldn't classify that prick as a person, but he's an actual being, yes," Wolf answers.

"This," Arlo starts, pressing a hand to her forehead and walking a couple paces away from us. "This is all so much. Too much."

Kane moves to her, pulling her into his arms and she goes willingly, burying her face in the crook of his neck and gripping the material of the sweater at his back. "We can talk more about it tomorrow. Why don't we drive into town and get some dinner?"

"I could eat," Arlo says, her voice muffled by the skin of Kane's neck.

She's taken all this surprisingly well so far, which makes me scared about what can happen in the upcoming days. I promised her we would leave her alone if that's what she decides, but that's one promise I don't think I can keep.

Andréa Joy

CHAPTER SEVEN

ARLO

WE ALL SHUFFLE into Hunter's SUV since his is the bigger one and we can all fit comfortably. I'm in the back row, Wolf on one side and Kane on the other and I'm not even mad. Through all of this I've come to realize that I'm not as close to Wolf as I am the others and my chest aches with that knowledge. I rub a palm over my heart and lean slightly more into him. Wolf shifts and throws an arm around my shoulders, pulling me in closer.

"You okay, Little Lamb?"

My breath catches in my throat and the entire vehicle goes silent at the nickname. I haven't heard it since that night. Since Kane whispered it in my ear before… before… I swallow hard and press my face into Wolf's chest, squeezing my eyes shut and wishing the memories from that night would disappear.

"Shit," Wolf says, running his other hand down his face. "I wasn't thinking."

"No," I say, sitting up enough to comfortably look at him. "It's okay. I-I kind of missed hearing it, actually." A small smile pulls at the corners of my lips and Wolf relaxes again.

Even though the nickname triggers the memories from Halloween night, it also sends butterflies fluttering in my gut. It makes me feel special that they gave me a silly nickname. A nickname only used by the four of them. It's weird, I'm not experiencing any of the emotions I'm supposed to be feeling after going through what I did. Where there's supposed to be anger and resentment, there's just grieving. Grieving for the relationships that were lost that night. I'd be lying if I said that night made me fall out of love with these men. If I were to confess that to my girlfriends - that's if I had any - they would look at me like I was crazy. After all, shouldn't you immediately stop loving someone who tries to kill you? If there was a fine line between love and hate then shouldn't I hate them now after what they did? It's not like they lied or cheated. They. Tried. To. Kill. Me. And yet, here I am, hoping against all hope that we can move on from that night. What the fuck's wrong with me? Surely, there's something in my brain that's gone haywire. Despite all that, I find myself, laying my head in Wolf's lap while my feet rest on Kane's lap and I close my eyes for the drive in to town. Normal's overrated anyway, I think as I drift off to sleep.

Wolf wakes me a little while later when we pull into the parking lot of the restaurant. He strokes a hand down my hair making goosebumps pebble along my arms.

"Wake up, sleepy head," he croons in my ear.

I absently swat at him with my hand and snuggle in again to go back to sleep. Despite being all muscle, his lap is surprisingly comfortable. I think I've found my new favourite napping spot.

Someone chuckles close by. "I guess you're not that hungry then?"

Suddenly, I'm wide awake. I shoot back up to sitting and look around the now empty vehicle except for Wolf and me. Jagger laughs from outside the passenger side door on Wolf's side. "Someone said something about food," I say just as my stomach lets out a loud grumble.

Both Wolf's and Jagger's eyes grow comically wide at the sound. Heat creeps up my cheeks and I climb out the car on my side and round the back. I'm assuming Kane and Hunter are already in the restaurant since they're not out here so I take off toward the entrance leaving Wolf and Jagger to catch up behind me. There's no hostess waiting up front to greet us, but I immediately catch sight of Hunter and Kane anyway and make my way over to the table. I clear my throat as I scoot across the bench seat, a grin spreading across my face when the two of them break apart. Their lips both wet and swollen from the kiss they were just sharing.

"Have a nice nap?" Hunter asks, grinning. Kane blushes and scoots in closer to him as Jagger takes a seat on the other side.

"If I had known what I was missing in here, I would've woken up earlier," I say, my eyes bouncing between the two of them.

"Any time you want a show, Little Lamb, just say the word," Hunter says, grinning when I bite into my bottom lip.

"I might just have to."

The waitress comes to take our food and drink order. Her eyes move from me to each one of the guys in turn, one of her brows lifts in a silent question but then she shakes her head as if the answer is too outrageous to think about. When her eyes linger a little too long on Jagger, my fingers curl in a fist under the table, my nails digging into my palm until I'm sure I'll have little half-moon shapes indented in them. Wolf slides a hand over mine and gives a quick squeeze. He leans over so only I can hear his next words.

"She's got nothing on you, Little Lamb." His breath is warm against my ear making me shiver. I turn my head slightly, bringing our faces closer together.

Wolf's eyes drop down to my lips when I lick them. Like an invisible string pulling him closer, he leans the last couple inches separating us and kisses me.

It's not as demanding as Hunter's, or slow and romantic like Kane's, or exploratory like Jagger's. Wolf's kiss is comforting. It's coming home after a long day and slipping into your favourite pair of pajamas. It's a cup of hot chocolate on a cold night. It's knowing that there'll always be someone there to catch you when you fall. My breaths are quick pants when he finally pulls away, but only enough so he can see my face. His palm cups my face, his thumb tracing gently over my cheek bone as he gazes into my eyes and then kisses me again.

He jolts and breaks the connection, glaring at one of the guys across the table. "The fuck was that for?"

"We're in the middle of a damn restaurant," Hunter grumbles.

Confusion pulls Wolf's brows together before understanding dawns and a bright smile spreads across his face. "My bad," he says, and moves to right himself again.

"Fucking tease," Kane mumbles under his breath, making me giggle.

I may have momentarily forgot that the others were watching us from across the table but knowing that watching me kiss Wolf possibly turned them on is, well, it makes me feel like maybe I'm not so powerless in this relationship.

The waitress brings our food and we eat in relative quiet. I take a bite of my clubhouse sandwich and glance up to find Kane watching me, a mischievous smile pulling up the corners of his lips. He stretches out on the bench seat between Hunter and Jagger causing his leg to bump into mine. I bump his back as a blush works its way up my neck and blossoms across my cheeks. He leans forward, then, his hands disappear under the table. Kane traces gentle circles on my knees making me shiver and I take a sip of my drink to cover the moan threatening to spill passed my lips. His grin grows into something teasing as he continues his ministrations, his hands sliding higher up my legs until the top constricts his progress. God, that feels good. Wolf leans closer into my side, his palm landing warm and solid on my thigh as he continues his conversation with Hunter and Jagger across the table. The other two seemingly unaware of what Kane and Wolf are doing to me under it.

Wolf's palm slides closer down my thigh where Kane's hands have stopped. I feel them link fingers briefly before Wolf drags his palm up my inner thigh, stopping just before where I need him the most. He casts a quick glance in Kane's direction, some sort of secret message passing between the two of them before his hand starts up my thigh again. I lean slightly back against the plastic cushions and spread my legs wider, giving him better access. When he doesn't continue up higher, I fold my hand over his and bring it to where I want it. Wolf chokes on the french fry he just put in his mouth and when Hunter and Jagger's eyes snap to me, I plaster on an innocent smile and shrug like I have no idea what just happened. Both their eyes narrow like they're not buying it. Kane sits back again, taking his hands with him and stretches his arms above his head. The move causes his shirt to lift up just enough to expose a sliver of skin above the waistband of his jeans. My greedy eyes roam over the patch of hair that disappears down into his pants and I lick my lips.

A groan sounds from beside Kane and I realize that when he brought his arms down after stretching, his hands disappeared again but they're not on me like they were before. I glance over to Hunter, his teeth biting so hard into his bottom lips, it's turning the flesh white. I grin and look over to Jagger who's panting, his back plastered against the bench, and my grin grows wider. Wolf flips open the button on my pants, but I grab onto his wrist to stop him.

"I, uh, I think we should go back to the cabin."

I barely have the words out before Jagger's head is on a swivel looking for our waitress. Once he finds her, he jumps up and heads toward her, pulling his wallet from his back pocket. Hunter and Kane slide out of their bench, Wolf stands, adjusting the bulge in his pants, before offering me his hand. I giggle and slip my palm into his. A surprised yelp leaves me when he pulls me straight up into his chest, his arms stretching around me like a band.

"Proud of yourself, are you?" He says, leaning down to nip at the curve of my neck.

"Very, actually." I beam up at him.

Kane wraps an arm around my waist from behind and pulls me to him, causing Wolf to drop his hand. "Stop hogging our girl." He scowls, but the corner of his lips twitch like he's trying to hide his smile.

Wolf mumbles something under his breath that I can't understand, and then his hand is pressing against my lower back. Kane takes my hand and together the three of us walk back out to the vehicle to wait for Hunter and Jagger. I know Jagger went to pay the bill but I have no idea where Hunter disappeared to. When we get back to the SUV, Wolf unlocks the door with his phone and opens the back door. He grips me by my waist and lifts me up, depositing me on the back seat. Before he can pull away, I curl my legs around his body and my fingers into the front of his shirt. It's been months since I've had any of their hands on me and I just now realized how much I missed it.

"Arlo," he breathes. His voice rough and ragged.

The other passenger door opens and closes behind me and then Kane is sliding up against my back. He moves my hair off my shoulder and kisses down my neck, while his fingers caress down between my breasts. I moan and let my head drop against his shoulder as my legs tighten around Wolf.

"Are you going to give our Little Lamb what she wants, Wolf? Or are you going to keep denying her?" Kane asks, sliding his fingers down my torso to the front of my jeggings where the button is still open from earlier in the restaurant. He flattens his palm and slides his hand down between my pants, under my panties.

I moan, spreading my thighs wider. Wolf runs his hands up my legs while Kane rubs circles against my clit. His fingers curl into the waistband of my pants and panties and yanks them down my legs, wiggling them back and forth a bit to get them all the way off. Kane's fingers never leave my clit while Wolf removes my pants. When I'm completely naked from the waist down, Kane increases the pressure on my clit. My hips buck up. I need more.

"God, look at you," Wolf says in awe with his palms braced on each thigh, holding me open. "All spread for us where anyone can see."

I blush and try to close my legs a little, but Wolf doesn't allow it. He pushes my legs open again and then curls his arms around my thighs and pulls me until my ass is hovering on the edge of the seat. Kane moves with me and wraps his other arm around my middle, holding me up and making sure I don't slide out of the vehicle.

"Don't be shy, Little Lamb," Kane whispers in my ear. "They may look, but they'll never be able to touch."

Wolf leans down, spreading me open with his thumbs and then his lips close around my clit and suck. I cry out at the jolt of sensations. My back arches of its own accord, but Kane's arm around my middle pushes down, forcing me to drop back down and take whatever Wolf gives me. His nips gently at the ball of nerves and I shiver then moan when he licks up my slit.

Time and our surroundings cease to exist as Wolf licks me like I'm his favourite lollipop and Kane runs his roughs hands all over my torso, pinching my nipples every now and then to add to the dizzying sensations. I slide my fingers through Wolf's close-cropped hair and curl my fingers in the strands as my orgasm crashes into me. This time when I buck my hips and arch my back, they don't stop me.

Just as I'm coming down from my high, and Wolf helps Kane maneuver me into the backseat, I hear a voice say,

"Damn, that was hot." While another says, "I can't believe we fucking missed it."

Wolf and Kane chuckle close by, but I'm half asleep. The last thing I remember is Wolf pulling my feet into his lap while Kane caresses my hair.

CHAPTER EIGHT

ARLO

IT'S BEEN ALMOST a full week since that day at the restaurant, and while things have mostly gone back to normal between the five of us, I haven't fully forgiven them yet. But I'm working on it. It helped that they tried to explain to me why they had to do what they did. I still don't understand all of it, but they're helping me with that too. Every day I learn something new about The Elders and their history.

Speaking of history, I let out a relieved breath when I push open the lecture room doors after my Art History class and head over to the Student Services Center where I got a locker for the day. I needed a lot of textbooks for my classes today so instead of hauling them with me, I decided to drop them in one of the day use lockers until the end of the day. Jagger offered to drive me home after my classes so that I don't have to take the TTC with them or walk.

I've just opened the metal door when a piece of folded paper floats out and lands on the floor at my feet. I glance around to see who could've put it there, but nobody's paying me any attention. I deposit my books in the locker and then squat down to pick up the note.

I warned you to stay away from them. Your life is in danger.

Something taps my shoulder and I scream, dropping the note to cover my face from my attack.

"Hey," A familiar voice says, gripping my shoulders and spinning me around. "Arlo, what's going on?"

I lower my hands to find Wolf's face pulled into a concerned look as his eyes roam my own face and the rest of my body. Presumably looking for injuries. When I point to the note on the ground, he follows my finger and his brows pull down in a frown. His hands leave my shoulders only long enough so he can pick up the note and then he wraps an arm around my waist as he reads.

"What the fuck is this?"

"I-I don't know," I stammer, curling into his side and burying my face in his chest. Wolf's hand rubs my back in slow slides up and down. "I think it's the same guy who attacked me around the block from your house." It's the only explanation I have as to who it could be. He's the only one who's warned me to stay away from them.

"C'mon. Let's get you out of here." He grabs my books from the locker and stuffs them inside his backpack along with his own, before grabbing the lock and putting it in a side pocket. He swings the bag over his shoulder like it weighs nothing and then reaches for my hand, linking our fingers together as he leads us out the building and down to the main parking lot.

"And nobody was around when you found it?" Hunter asks, pacing the floor in front of the impressive fireplace.

It's the first time I've been inside their *library*. Library is putting it mildly. It reminds me of something you'd find at a gentlemen's club, but less obnoxious somehow.

"No one who looked like they could've been the guy from that night," Wolf says from my one side.

I haven't contributed much to this conversation. I'm still partly rattled from finding the note in my locker earlier and still partly surprised by the magnificence of this room. I'm actually in awe that this room exists in a house that looks like this one from the outside. I mean, this isn't my first time inside their house but I don't ever remember a room like this.

"Little Lamb," Kane subtly nudges my arm from my other side, jolting me out of my wonderings.

"Huh?"

The guys chuckle at my deer-in-headlights expression. Hunter runs a hand over his mouth to hide his smile but not before I see the sides twitch up.

"You need to call him," Jagger says, his eyes turning serious as he looks back at Hunter. The other guys nod in agreement but Hunter shakes his head.

"Absolutely not. There's nothing he can do anyway," he answers, but his attention is on the note laying on the desk in front of him. I hadn't even noticed that he had stopped his pacing.

"Who?" I ask.

Turquoise eyes look up at me from under long, dark lashes, but they're not as bright as I'm used to seeing them. There's a haunted look in them now. Hunter sighs, running a hand down his face and bracing his hands on his hips. "Hades."

Shocked, I accidentally blurt, "Like, your ex?"

Hunter drops his chin to his chest and exhales hard, his shoulders actually deflating from the move.

"He can lend us Cerberus," Wolf suggests. "I miss that mutt."

"Fuck no," Jagger interjects, cringing and feigning a shudder. "He slobbers everywhere."

Kane laughs so hard he's bent over, one arm wrapped around his belly with his other hand braced on the opulent desk.

"I still don't know how you didn't realize that your underwear was wet *before* you put it on."

I giggle, and then choke it down when Jagger turns his glare on me. I have to bury my face in Wolf's chest to stop myself from laughing.

"I was half asleep," Jagger grumbles.

"Wet undergarments aside," Hunter says, "I'm not asking for Hades help again." He starts pacing again and then plops down in one of the four wingback chairs. "What if we do it the old-fashioned way or call Gabriel or Tron."

Just like Hunter objected to speaking to Hades, now it's Wolf who objects. "We're not calling Metatron."

"Wait, Metatron?" I ask, looking up at Wolf like he just made that name up. "Sounds like a robot or a character in a video game."

His lips quirk up in a crooked grin. "He's the Angel of the written word and the record keeper. There isn't anything that someone can do on Earth that he doesn't have a record of."

My cheeks heat thinking about what three of us did in the parking lot of that restaurant last week. "Oh."

"He also knows the intentions behind what someone writes. He would be a good resource in this case," Kane adds.

"No. Find another way," Wolf insists, which causes every eye in the room to turn his way.

"Me thinks you doth protest too much," Jagger quips, then ducks when Wolf tosses a book at his head.

"Me thinks you want to get your ass kicked… again," Wolf bites.

"Alright, boys," I say, patting Wolf's chest. "When you're ready, I'd like to hear that story, but for now—" I turn my attention back to Hunter. "Is there any other way without getting Hades and Metatron involved?" *How is this my life?* I'm sure it won't be the last time I ask myself this question.

Hunter works his jaw back and forth a couple times and then leans forward to rest his elbows on his knees. "Like Wolf said, we try doing it the old fashion way. I'll see if I can get someone to run the fingerprints."

"Another ex?" I mumble, a bit miffed.

Hunter grins, standing up and closing the distance between us. He doesn't pull me out from under Wolf's arm but lifts my chin with two of his fingers so that I'm forced to meet his stare.

"Jealousy looks good on you."

"I'm not jealous," I lie.

Hunter leans in until his lips brush the shell of my ear. "You're fucking sexy when you're jealous. If I didn't have to leave right now, I would take you upstairs and show you that you have nothing to worry about. My dick only gets hard for the people in this room." I shiver as he pulls away to meet my eyes again, the blue-green colour now completely black from lust.

"Promise?" I pull my bottom lip between my teeth and chew on the flesh.

Hunter tugs on my bottom lip with the thumb from the hand still on my chin. Then he's taking it between his own teeth and biting down. My breath hitches at the slight sting of pain, but when he sucks my lip into his mouth, I moan. He pulls away all too quickly and I pout.

"Don't worry, H," Wolf says, tightening his arm around me. "We'll keep her entertained until you get back."

"Actually," Kane cuts in, stepping up beside Hunter. "Jagger and I will go with you. These two," he tips his head to indicate Wolf and I, "Haven't had much time to bond."

The three of them leave and then it's just Wolf and I alone in the big room. He laughs, moving me in front of him and curling both arms around my waist.

"I'm not going to eat you."

"Actually…" I run my hands up his chest and over his broad shoulders to link them behind his neck. "I was thinking I might like a repeat of last week."

His already dark brown eyes darken even more. His hand cups the side of my face, his fingers threading through my hair. "Is that the only thing you were hoping for?" His voice comes out rough. The sound going straight between my legs.

"No," I breathe, pulling his face down closer. "It's just the start." I close the last couple inches and fuse my lips with his, drinking him in.

Wolf groans, running his hands down my back to cup my ass. He lifts me up and my legs wrap around his waist as he walks us out of the library and up the stairs to his bedroom. Disappointment at not doing it on the desk downstairs settles in my gut for a split second until I'm being deposited on the soft mattress and Wolf follows me down, hovering above me.

It takes us no time at all to shed our clothes. I climb on top of him and trace the lines of his abs with my tongue before going on to trace the tattoos on each of his pecks. Wolf groans, bending his knees to brace his feet on the bed behind me. His cock slides between my slit with the move. Time ceases to exist for us in this moment. It's just him and I finding our way together amidst the chaos of what our lives have become in such a short amount of time. Just as we find our own orgasms, I feel our bond strengthen and solidify.

CHAPTER NINE

"WHAT DID YOU guys find out?"

I pull Arlo down onto my lap on the couch. She giggles but snuggles into my chest while still making sure that she can see the other guys. Kane drops down beside me and pulls her feet into his lap for a foot massage.

Jagger sits on the arm of the chair Hunter's sitting in. Hunter's hand immediately goes to Jagger's lower back and the two of them share a look before turning to face the rest of us. Even though we're able to communicate with each other telepathically, they've been too far for me to hear them until now.

Hunter: We don't know if she'll be able to handle what we found out.

Me: What is it?

Arlo looks between all of us, her brows scrunching down in the middle. "Did you guys say something?"

My hand pauses where I've been lightly drawing shapes into one of her thighs.

Jagger: There's no way.

Kane: Can she?

"Okay, what's going on?" Arlo says, pulling her feet from Kane's lap and sitting up in mine so she's no longer leaning into my chest.

I clear my throat and swallow hard, unsure where to even begin. "What did you hear?"

She looks from me to Kane to Jagger before settling on Hunter. "You said you weren't sure if I'd be able to handle what you found out." She frowns, biting down on a corner of her bottom lip. "Didn't you?"

We all turn our attention to Hunter, waiting with bated breath to take our cues from him. We had assumed things would change once we all solidified our bonds with Arlo. The thought of her being able to communicate with us this way was not one of those things.

Jagger stands from his seat and comes to kneel in front of Arlo. I help her turn in my lap so her back is to my chest, and Jagger takes her hands in his.

"I'm going to try something, okay?" He asks and she nods, still confused about what's going on.

Jagger: Can you hear me?

I roll my eyes. Real smooth. *Can you hear me now*, I mimic and catch a back hand on the arm from Arlo. I look at her, shocked.

"I could hear both of you. What's going on? Why can I hear your voices in my head?" She yanks her hands from Jagger and he straightens, taking a few steps back to allow her room to scramble off my lap. "Is this part of your gifts?"

"Yes," Kane says, standing. As soon as he moves towards Arlo, she backs up a step so he stops and holds his hands up, palms out.

"But why," she pauses. "Why can *I* hear you?"

Hunter and I stand at the same time and join the others in a make-shift circle with us on one side and Arlo on the other.

"We didn't know this would happen," Hunter says. "But I think—" He looks from Arlo to me and back again before continuing, "I think once you and Wolf got closer, it changed our bond somehow." Hunter's eyes narrow as he studies Arlo a lot closer than I've seen him study anyone in a long time. I'm about to ask him what exactly they found today when he begins speaking again. "What do you know about your father?"

Arlo jerks back like Hunter slapped her but she doesn't take any more steps away from us. "What? Why?"

Out of the corner of my eye, I see Kane look to Hunter who gives him a clipped nod. Kane steps forward and this time Arlo doesn't take a step back. It feels like the four of us break out a collective relieved breath.

"You know how humanity wasn't created to be alone? That people were created for community and to pair up and procreate?" Kane asks.

Arlo nods. "Yeah."

"Well," Jagger jumps in. "It's the same for us. We were meant to be a five not four."

"We're not the first Horsemen to walk the Earth," I add and Arlo's eyes grow wide.

"There was another group before us. But before they could find their fifth, one of them fell in love with a mortal, so to speak," Hunter says.

"What happened?" Arlo asks, seemingly more invested in the story now.

"We don't know the full story, but there were rumours that the other three despised the fourth for falling in love. They tried to kill him and the woman he fell in love with, but he somehow managed to hide them both for a couple years."

Arlo raises a shaky hand to cover her mouth. After a few moments, she asks, "Did they find them?"

Hunter, Jagger, Kane, and I share a look before turning our attentions back to Arlo. "We don't know," I answer, truthfully. "But we do know that they had a child."

"A child they were able to cloak for over almost two decades," Kane adds.

Finally, Hunter steps closer to Arlo and repeats his question from earlier, but gentler this time. "What do you know about your dad, Little Lamb?"

She shrugs, wrapping her arms around herself. When Kane steps closer and pulls her into his arms, she doesn't fight it. In fact, she leans in closer to him.

"Not much," she says. "I was six when he died on deployment. I remember he was in the Canadian Navy. I remember he used to come home and lift me up to sit on his shoulders as he zoomed around the house pretending to be an airplane. I—" She stops, lifting her gaze to look at all of us. "Was he the four? Was the woman he fell in love with my mom?"

"We don't know," Hunter says. "But the fingerprints on the note left in your locker came back as a match to Joseph Williams."

"My dad was the one who attacked me that night?" Her voice rises part way through as a panicked look crosses her face.

"Again, we don't know. It's not hard to transfer a set of fingerprints."

"But," she says, watching Hunter closely.

"But," he says, "My contact seems to think that it wasn't transferred."

Arlo blows out a harsh breath. She turns out of Kane's arms and walks to the other side of the room to stare out the window. The sun set hours ago so it's pitch black out, but I don't think that matters to her right now. I'm sure we're all thinking the same thing. Why would he start showing up now? Why start leaving notes and fingerprints behind when everyone's believed him to be dead for almost thirteen years.

"If that was him then why would he be warning me away from you guys? He must know that you're nothing like the oth--" She stops talking and spins away from the window, her eyes wide. "Wait, The Elders, are they the other three?"

"That's the assumption we've been operating under. No-one else knows about our existence."

"Well, no one on Earth," I say, clarifying Hunter's comment.

Something heavy settles in the air around us. Anticipation. Frustration. Hurt. Anger. It feels like a mix of all those and more. Finally, Kane breaks the tension.

"Enough of the heavy shit for tonight. Someone has a big birthday coming up."

Arlo snorts. "I hardly think my birthday should take precedence over all this," she says, waving a hand to indicate all of us.

"You only turn twenty once, Little Lamb. All this other stuff will still be there," Jagger says, walking back into the room with his hands full of drinks. I hadn't even noticed he had left, that's how focused I was on our girl.

"Is there anything special you'd like to do?" I ask, sliding my hands into my pockets to prevent myself from reaching for her. Now that I know what she feels like beneath my hands, I've been counting down the minutes until I can have her again.

"Honestly?" She blows out a breath, sending a lock of hair floating up in the air. "I haven't really thought about it."

"Well, you have a week to figure it out," Hunter says, tipping back the drink Jagger handed him. "Right now, though, I think it's time for all of us to go to bed. It's been a long day."

With murmurs of agreement, we all throw back our drinks and put the glasses on the coffee table to be cleaned up tomorrow before heading to the stairs. Arlo pauses on the landing at the top, her gaze roaming over all the doors. I grin, taking her hand in mine and pulling her along with me to the fifth bedroom. It used to be a guest room, but we've recently redecorated. As soon as I push open the door, Arlo's jaw drops open. Kane wraps his arms around her from behind and places a kiss on her shoulder.

"The five of us would never be able to fit in Hunter's bed," Kane says, walking Arlo further into the room while the other two follow behind.

Hunter closes the door behind him. We all strip and crawl into bed with Arlo in the middle.

Andréa Joy

CHAPTER TEN

ARLO

"MY DAD IS alive or could still possibly be alive," is the only thing that's been playing through my mind ever since last night. We don't know for sure if he's the one that attacked me that night and left the note in my locker; although, the fact that his fingerprints were on the note is a pretty big indicator that he's alive.

I wiggle around until I can turn on my side and cuddle up to Wolf. Hunter automatically moves in closer behind me, but the little snores puffing against the back of my head tell me that he's still asleep. Amidst finding out that my dad is still alive, I'm still trying to wrap my head around the fact that these four aren't who I originally thought they were. They're not even human. I wiggle around again, trying to find a comfortable spot between two men who are roughly the size of linebackers.

"Little Lamb, if you don't quit moving around I'm going to tire you out until you pass out," Wolf grunts beneath my cheek.

I raise my eyes to his without moving from my spot and grin. "Promise?"

His arm wraps around me and pulls until I'm spread out on top of him. Wolf grips my hips and maneuvers me into a more comfortable position for both of us and curls a hand around the side of my neck. "You doubt my abilities?" He nips my jaw then presses a kiss to the same spot.

I shiver, digging the pads of my fingers into the skin on his chest. He has a light smattering of dark hair on his chest just like Hunter, but it's courser. Remembering the way it rubbed against my back as he took me from behind last night, as my hips grind down on his.

"Arlo," he growls, but I'm not sure if it's in warning or a plea.

Either way, I lift up just enough to get my hand between our bodies as I take hold of his dick and angle it at my opening. I slide down his length after removing my hand and sit up straighter, taking him deeper. Wolf groans beneath me, his hands finding my hips and gripping them as I begin to rock back and forth on his dick.

"Jesus," someone breathes. I look to the left to see Kane has rolled over onto his back and the waistband of his boxers are pulled down below his balls. His fist is wrapped around his hard cock while his eyes are locked onto the place where Wolf and I are joined.

"Fucking hell," Jagger says when he wakes up and realizes what's going on at the same time Hunter groans a drawn out, "Fuuck."

All of a sudden a second pair of hands are on my hips and I'm in the air before landing on my back in the middle of the Alaskan King mattress. Hunter pulls on my panties until they rip then tosses them somewhere behind him. He wedges my legs further apart and lying on his stomach, licks a strip up my slit. His tongue circles my clit a few times before his lips close around the nub and he sucks. I arch my back, pushing my head further into the pillow and moan but it's cut off when Wolf lifts my head and pushes the head of his cock passed my lips. I curl my fingers around the base and greedily pull him in deeper, swallowing him to the back of my throat.

Two more sets of hands begin caressing my body. Sliding up, down, and around my torso while playing with my breasts and pinching and twisting my nipples every so often. I moan around Wolf's length and thread my fingers through Hunter's hair, letting my knees drop open to the side and bucking my hips up to meet each slide of his fingers. The bed dips and shakes as Hunter moves over to make room for Kane and then both their mouths are licking and sucking me. At one point I even think they both have fingers inside of me, I'm stretched so full.

Wolf curses above me, his dick sliding from my lips. I tighten my fingers around his base and press a kiss to the head before letting him go.

"Think you can take two of us again, Little Lamb?" Hunter asks, moving to his knees and wiping his chin.

My whole face heats at the move and the grin that spread across his face at my reaction is wicked.

"Please." The word sounds like a plea on my lips.

Wolf lays down on the bed again and pulls me back on top of him. I slide easily down his cock until he's buried to the hilt. He takes my face between his hands and pulls me down for a kiss until my chest is plastered to his. A firm hand presses against my back until there's nothing separating Wolf and I, and then the head of another cock is pressing in right alongside Wolf's. A hand wraps itself in my long hair and pulls me off Wolf's lips, forcing me to look over my shoulder. My eyes connect with Hunter's for a split second before his lips are replacing Wolf's. Hunter's tongue licks along the seam of my lips and I happily open for him, groaning when he sucks my tongue into his mouth.

The bed dips again. This time it's because Kane is standing at my hips. He waits for Hunter to lean back as far as he can before he plants one foot on the side of me but in front of Hunter.

"Ow! What was that for?" Kane squeals, one hand pressed against his ass cheek as he looks back at Hunter who's grinning.

"You have a biteable butt."

Kane harrumphs, but squats down, running the already lubed head of his cock against my ass. I freeze, not sure if I'm ready for that again yet, but Wolf's soothing hands on my body and Jagger's whispered words in my ear help me relax enough for Kane to slide passed the muscle. It still stings from lack of prep and I feel a bit uncomfortable from the fullness, but soon, when Kane and Hunter begin to move it all blends into something I have no words for. Wolf grunts, his hands on my hips tightening and Kane grabs hold of my shoulder while the fingers of his other hand intertwine with Wolf's at my hip.

"C'mere," I tell Jagger, hating to leave him out.

He shuffles until his knees are planted on the bed on either side of Wolf's head. I take him into my mouth easily and try to set a rhythm but can't quite keep it up as Hunter, Wolf, and Kane set a pace that has my eyes rolling into the back of my head and I moan around Jagger's length. Eventually, he fists a hand in my hair and fucks my face. I don't think I can hold out anymore. It's all too much. Too much sensations happening all at once, my body feels overwhelmingly sensitive.

Jagger's hand in my hair tightens almost painfully. His body stutters and then he's moaning out Wolf's and my names before spurts of hot cum spill down my throat. I try to swallow it all but some leaks out the sides. When Jagger pulls out, I lick my lips to collect the remnants.

"Fuck, that's hot," Jagger groans, bending down to lick along my bottom lip and then kisses me.

Wolf comes next, gripping my hips harder and surging up with a low growl. His release must have triggered Hunter's who comes with a, "Fuck. Fuck. Fuck."

And then hot cum fills my ass as Kane's orgasm washes over him. I collapse on top of Wolf's chest, my legs all wobbly and not able to keep me up anymore. The other guys move off the bed to presumably clean up. I'm almost half asleep again when a tongue licks a trail from my pussy to my ass. I groan and wiggle back into it.

"Kane," Jagger groans from somewhere to the side. "At least give us a few minutes to recover if you're going to lick the cum out of her holes."

I move my head to the side to see both Jagger and Hunter start to harden again at the sight of Kane cleaning me up with his tongue. He grunts but doesn't stop until he's gotten every last drop. Then his tongue is being replaced by a warm wash cloth. I sigh into Wolf's chest and close my eyes, drifting off again with the knowledge that I have all my men here with me.

Andréa Joy

CHAPTER ELEVEN

ARLO

"WELL, YOU TWO look awfully cozy." Jules beams as she walks down the hallway towards Kane and I.

He wraps an arm around my shoulders and pulls me in closer to his side, placing a kiss on the top of my head.

"Gross," Jules says, feigning disgust at seeing her stepbrother kiss her best friend.

I giggle and playfully slap Kane's chest and then move away to pull Jules into a tight hug. God, I've missed this woman. I feel like a shitty friend for avoiding her when the stuff with the guys went down but I couldn't chance running into them then.

"I'm sorry," I whisper in her ear before pulling away.

She shrugs, a small, sad smile on her face. "It's okay. I get it, but one of these days we need to chat about what happened."

"Deal," I say, pulling her into a second hug and making her giggle. "By the way, I'm loving the pink hair."

"Right!? I think I like it better than the blue I had over Christmas break." She twirls a section of hair around her fingers, but her smile is bright. She looks happy.

"Are you staying for your last class or coming over?" Kane asks, pulling me back into him by my hips and nuzzling the side of my neck.

I tip my head to the side to give him more access, and pout. "I already have a midterm so I should go."

"What? That's crazy! It's still the first month back," Jules says in shock.

"I know. That's what I said. We have two midterms and then the final. But at least the final is worth less, so," I shrug as best I can while Kane's arms are around me. "I guess it works out."

"Nope," Jules says, walking along side us as Kane walks me to my last class of the day. "I'd rather do a final paper than a second midterm."

"You and me both," I agree just as we come to a stop outside the classroom.

Kane kisses me goodbye and lets me know that one of the guys will be picking me up after class. When him and Jules turn to walk away I'm almost tempted to take the failing grade on the midterm and go with them. The note in the locker is really messing with my head. I spent all week and weekend at their house because I was afraid of taking the train back to my place and being alone. But I can't keep living my life in fear, wondering where the next attack or note is going to come from. And honestly, it's a bit ridiculous that I'm afraid of my own father. I mean, he's my dad, what do I have to be afraid of?

You haven't known him in thirteen years. He could be different. Or maybe he wasn't who you thought he was. The guys aren't.

I shake off the thought and take a deep breath, entering the classroom only to stop short within steps of the door when my eyes connect with a familiar pair.

"What are you doing here?" I hurriedly sit down in the seat beside him before the girl eyeing him up and down like he's a snack can get a chance to take it.

Jagger grins, curling a hand around the nape of my neck and pulling me in for a kiss. What I thought was going to be a quick peck turns into something that should not be safe around prying eyes, especially ones belonging to first year students who are still in the high school mentality. Even so, I couldn't care less as I kiss Jagger back just as passionately.

"Hi," he whispers against my lips when we finally break apart.

"Hi," I reply back and kiss him again before sitting back in my seat. I glance toward the girl and am met by a glare so icy that if it could, I would be a frozen sculpture ready for her to smash into tiny pieces. Holding her gaze, I let the corner of my lips tip up into a smirk and reach a hand over to run through Jagger's hair. I've been loving the longer strands on him ever since he decided to grow it out last semester. He has a sort of Jax Teller look about him now.

"Hunter's right," Jagger says, leaning in close so only I can hear him. "Jealousy does look good on you, Little Lamb."

"I have no idea what you're talking about."

Jagger chuckles softly and takes my hand that was in his hair, bringing it down to press a kiss into my palm and then putting it on his thigh as the prof begins the midterm.

"So, let me get this straight," I say, as Jagger slips his palm against mine and laces our fingers together as we leave the classroom. "You're all going to take turns making sure I'm not alone throughout the day?"

My head's still pounding from the midterm we just had. I have no idea how Jagger did since he's missed every class before today, but it didn't seem too bad. I mean, it sucked, but I guess it could've been worse. I'm hopeful that he did okay, and if not, well, that's what study dates are for.

"We think it's for the best. At least until we can figure out what your dad knows and why he's suddenly decided to come out of hiding. Plus, with Adrian…" Jagger trails off, his eyes widen in horror for a split second before he covers the reaction with a cough and shake of his head. "We just don't want anything to happen to you."

"Wait, what about Hunter's dad?"

We stop outside of Jagger's Jeep. He gives me a puzzled look; his head tipped to the side and his brows furrowing in the middle.

"Adrian? Hunter's dad and my mom's boyfriend?" I clarify.

"He's not… He's… I mean…"

I haven't see Jagger this flustered in, well, since I've known him. We climb into the vehicle but before he can start the engine, I shift in my seat so I can face him and lay a hand on his arm. "What's going on? What aren't you telling me?"

He opens his mouth to say something and then closes it again, mumbling something under his breath that I can't make out.

"Let's go back to our place and we'll tell you everything we know."

Not at all satisfied with that answer but knowing it's the best I'm going to get for right now, I turn around in my seat to put my seatbelt on, but I catch sight of a figure standing in front of the Jeep and gasp. Jagger's head shoots up from where he was looking at his phone and curses.

"Seatbelt. Now."

I scramble to get the belt secured as Jagger floors it out of the parking stall and squeals out of the parking lot, taking the corner on two wheels. We've barely cleared the parking lot when I hear Jagger's voice in my head demanding the others meet us at the house.

"Who was that?" I ask, looking back over my shoulder to see if the man I saw is following us, but I don't see anything. There's not even any traffic.

Jagger's jaw twitches as he clenches his teeth. Not saying a word. The tires screech as we pull into their driveway and Jagger cuts the engine. As soon as I slide from the passenger seat, he grabs my hand in his again and hurries us inside.

"What the fuck's going on?" Wolf asks, coming to a stop in front of us. From his laboured breathing, I'm guessing he must have just got back from a run.

Hunter and Kane appear behind him, wearing matching concerned looks.

Jagger ignores Wolf's question and looks to Hunter. "You need to call Hades now."

Before the words have fully left Jagger's lips, Hunter starts shaking his head. "Absolutely not—"

"We saw an Aqrabuamelu," Jagger adds, interrupting whatever Hunter was about to say.

Wolf, Kane, and Hunter's faces all instantly drain of color at the name.

"What's a aqra-whatever-whatever?" I ask, waving my hand in the air.

The guys stare each other down until Kane eventually says, "It's a mythical creature. Half human and half scorpion." To Jagger he says, "Are you sure?"

"I only caught a quick glimpse of it, but I'm pretty damn sure. Unless I imagined the scorpion tail."

"Fucking hell," they all utter at once.

I'm still utterly confused. Half human, half scorpion? Again, how is this my life? I feel like I went to sleep and woke up in an altered dimension where Angels, Mythical Creatures, and the Devil freely walk the earth, while the majority of the world is oblivious but I somehow got blessed - or cursed - with this knowledge. I watch my men talk things out amongst themselves as I quietly stand to one side, not wanting to get in their way. No matter what happens, I can't think of meeting these guys as a curse. Where my life was boring, they give me adventure. Where I only ever had my mom, they give me love and acceptance.

Hunter's exasperated sigh brings me out of my thoughts. "Alright, I'll get in touch with him while you guys grab a couple bags. We'll stop at Arlo's condo before heading to the cabin."

"What? Why?" I'm not ready to go back to that place again. It was bad enough when I met them up there several weeks ago, but I hadn't ever planned on going back.

"We're safer out there," Jagger says, stepping around me to go into the library and coming out with an arm full of books. "The Elders have been known to use Dybbuks to carry out their dirty work. There are too many people in the city for us to stay here and risk that happening. Especially after what we saw today."

"Dybbuks?" I ask, my head spinning.

"A lost soul of a deceased person possessing the body of a living human until it's carried out its goal," Kane explains, jogging down the stairs with a duffel bag in each hand. He hands the bags over to Wolf when he remerges from the door leading to the garage. With his hands now free, Kane pulls me into a hug and kisses the top of my head. "Everything's going to be okay." The tension in my body instantly melts away the minute I catch a whiff of his scent. It's like he knew what I needed before I did. He pulls away and presses a hand to the small of my back to get me moving again. "We'll load into Hunter's

SUV in the garage while Wolf and Jagger take Jagger's Jeep and follows behind us."

In the garage, I immediately gravitate towards Wolf and fold my arms around his waist after he's put the bags in the back of Hunter's SUV. He hugs me back just as fiercely. His biceps almost as big as my face.

"We'll be right behind you, Little Lamb," he says into the top of my hair.

"Promise?" I haven't quite wrapped my head around what it means having these creatures appear, but my brain knows it's not good. And the thought of possibly losing one of my men has my stomach churning and nausea bubbling up my throat.

Wolf takes my face in his hands and leans down to kiss me. My fingers curl in the back of his shirt and I lift onto my tip toes to deepen the kiss.

"I won't ever leave you," his voice says in my head.

He gives me another squeeze and lets me go to help me into the SUV and then him and Jagger are making a run for Jagger's Jeep parked in the driveway.

"You guys have been here for over a century. Isn't there another remote place we can go that's not the cabin? I mean, how safe can it be if the Elders know about it?" I ask, as Hunter backs the SUV out of the garage and down the driveway.

Hunter and Kane exchange some sort of silent communication in the front seat before Kane shrugs. "We've always just automatically gone to the cabin but—"

"Does Tron still have that place up in Utterson?"

"I think so," Kane says, pulling out his phone. "Wolf's not going to be happy. You remember the last time he went up there?"

"I don't care. He'll get over it. We just need a place to lay low for a few weeks," Hunter says, taking a right turn onto my street. "Kane and Wolf will go with you to pack a bag. Jagger and I will wait and keep the vehicles running." Hunter glances at me in the rear-view mirror. An apology in his eyes. I'm not sure what he's trying to apologize for, though. For staying down here? For awaking me to all of this?

Kane opens my door and I take his hand as I step down on the running board and then down on the side walk. Jagger pulls up behind Hunter seconds later and then Wolf is joining us as we head into the lobby of my building and into the elevator.

Three and a half hours plus two snack stops later, we finally arrive at the cabin Kane and Hunter managed to get us last minute. As soon as Hunter pulls the SUV to a stop in front of the garage, I open my door and hop out. I spin in a slow circle taking in the barren trees and snow-covered ground. I stop and spot a clearing through some evergreen trees behind the house. It looks like there may be a lake down there in the warmer months, but it's currently frozen and covered in snow. Hunter, Wolf, and Jagger grab all of our bags from the vehicles while Kane leads me inside.

The little bungalow cabin didn't look like much from the outside, but the inside is incredible. I immediately feel the warmth from the wood fireplace as we step through the front door. Someone must have beaten us up here and gotten the fire started for us. There are hardwood floors through the main areas of the cabin. A plush area rug lays in the middle of the living room floor, in front of the fireplace and I can't help but imagine a cold night in front of the fire, a couple bottles of wine and the five us taking our time exploring each other's bodies. There are four bedrooms and one and a half bathrooms in the cabin, but neither bedroom has a bed big enough for all of us. I enter the biggest bedroom and sit on the foot of the queen bed, running my socked feet lightly over the carpet beneath them. This place is amazing. Almost majestic in its placement in nature. Yet I can't help but have this feeling of foreboding. Something tells me this isn't going to turn out to be the getaway the guys had planned for us and maybe we're not as isolated out here as we seem to think.

"Hey." Kane pokes his head in and raps his knuckles on the door frame. "You okay?"

I try to arrange my mouth in some sort of smile and clasp my hands together between my legs. "Yeah, All good."

He tips his head to the side to indicate the door on the other side of the hallway. "The other room has a queen bed and a sofa bed. We might have to get set up in there unless we want to split up."

"No," I say, pushing to my feet. The feeling of dread curling like a serpent in my gut at the thought of being separated from any of them even for a night. "We'll stay in that one then."

Kane looks at me strangely. When he opens his mouth to speak, I reach up on my toes and press my lips to his. It takes him awhile to react but when he does he curls one hand around my nape and the other around my waist. I have no choice but to hold on for the ride as he kisses me like it'll be the last time he'll ever have the chance to. We're both breathless and panting by the time we pull away, but he doesn't release his hold on me.

"I should go help Jagger with dinner," he eventually says. His lips brush against mine with each word. "There's a hot tub on the deck if you want to relax for a bit."

I bite my lip and Kane's eyes immediately drop down to my lips. His arm around my waist tightens. "I'll help in the kitchen then we can all enjoy the hot tub after dinner."

"I like the way you think." He pulls away only enough so his eyes can track down my body. I shiver and pray that dinner goes by fast.

Andréa Joy

CHAPTER TWELVE

I GRUMBLE AROUND THE kitchen as I get the dishes washed and put away while the others get changed and set up the hot tub.

Completely blindsided, that's what I was.

"You should take a nap if you want, I'm fine," he said.

The man knows how much I like to nap on road trips. I can't believe he used that shit against me. I woke up just as we were entering the city of Utterson, but it still didn't dawn on me where we were until we pulled onto the road that leads up to this cabin. Tron has made some changes since the last time we were up here. He added on two extra bedrooms and built the deck out on the back of the cabin and added a seven-person hot tub. But the rest is still as I remember it. I know that if it were warmer and I looked out the window above the kitchen sink, I would get a beautiful view of Three Mile Lake. I know that just to the left of the newly built-out deck is a hammock and a few feet in front of the hammock are about sixty stairs that lead down to the dock and the lake. There's also a small shed built into the side of the hill that houses kayaks, canoes, paddle boards, and any other water activity equipment. Tron always liked spending his days out on the water.

I curse and accidentally slam a plate down on the counter. After checking that it didn't crack or break, I put it in the cupboard with the others and close the door before folding the dish towel over the oven door handle. I never told the guys what happened between Tron and me because it was back when we were still seeing and sleeping around with other people. But Tron… he was different. I actually fancied myself falling for him. Until he dropped the bomb that I would never be what he wants in a relationship.

"You're not an Angel anymore, Wolf. You're not even a Guardian. You failed. A relationship between us will never work, but," he says, sliding up beside me and kissing up my neck. *"That doesn't mean we can't continue what we have."*

I was good enough to fuck, but not good enough to love. I sigh, bracing my hands on either side of the sink and let my head fall forward. It's just as well that we had ended it then. Not long after that, the four of us agreed we didn't want anyone else in our beds. And it wasn't long after *that* that we felt the shift and saw our Little Lamb. If anything, I should be thanking Tron for saying what he said. If he hadn't crushed me with those words then I wouldn't have agreed to stop seeing other people and we might not have Arlo with us now. Even if the circumstances could be better.

Speaking of Arlo, her laughter on the back deck draws me out of my memories and I look up to see her ducking behind the trunk of a tree as Jagger aims a snowball her way. Shaking all memories of Tron and this cabin off, I head outside to join the others. The other guys already managed to get the top off the hot tub and the jets started so without waiting for anyone, I strip down completely and get in, making sure to lift my glass a little higher so water doesn't get in it. Once I'm seated, I take a sip of the whiskey and set the glass on a nearby table that I can reach easily from my spot in the tub.

Arlo's jaw is still hanging open from where it dropped when I, well… dropped my drawers. I grin and motion her forward with a crook of my finger.

"It's nothing you haven't seen before, Little Lamb." I grin as a deep crimson blush blooms its way across her cheeks and down her neck.

"I-I know that," she stutters, adorably.

Hunter smirks, shaking his head and then he too strips down to nothing and joins me in the hot tub.

"You bring enough of those out here for all of us?" He asks, tipping his chin to indicate the glass I just put down.

"Nah, you fuckers left me in there to do the dishes alone. You can get your own drinks."

He rolls his eyes before turning to Jagger. "Can you get me a drink, J?" He flashes those pearly whites in a crooked grin and winks. I have to hide my amusement behind my hand.

When it comes to Hunter, Jagger is a sucker for that crooked grin and wink.

Jagger mumbles something I can't quite make out but then goes back inside the house, presumably to get Hunter his drink and the ones Arlo and Kane call out behind him. Kane joins Hunter and I in the hot tub which just leaves Arlo.

"Get your sexy ass in this hot tub before I come get you," Hunter growls from the seat beside me.

The deep timber of his voice makes my cock twitch and begin to take notice of the fact that I'm in a hot tub with two extremely sexy and naked men while we wait for our girl to join us. Arlo's eyes follow my hand as I trail it down the trimmed dusting of hair at my chest. She pulls her bottom lip between her teeth and bites down when my hand disappears below the surface of the water.

"Are you just going to stand there?" Kane asks.

She crosses her arms at her waist and lifts the long-sleeved shirt she's wearing painfully slowly until it's slipping past her fingers and landing in the snow. As soon as she steps out of her jeans and kicks off her shoes, Hunter stands up, water sleuthing down his toned body. Arlo squeals as he grabs her by the hips, lifts her up, and hauls her into the hot tub. Water splashes everywhere and Arlo harrumphs, crossing her arms over her chest and eyeing Hunter with a raised brow.

He shrugs, sitting down beside me again. "You were taking too long." I reach around him to trace circles on his opposite shoulder with a finger.

Jagger rejoins us and we all breathe out a collective sigh as the water bubbles around us from the jets and the heat seeps into our muscles.

"So," Arlo says, after finishing off her second glass of whiskey. There's a slight glassy look to her grey eyes already and a flush to her cheeks that I don't think's caused by the hot water. Our girl is well on her way to being sloshed. "What's the deal with the scorpion man." She leans further back against the edge of the hot tub and braces her arms on the side. I reach down under the water and grab her ankle, pulling her foot into my lap for a foot rub.

Kane squirms on his side of the hot tub but settles when Hunter reaches over and clasps a hand on his shoulder.

"The original story was that the Aqrabuamelu were created to wage a war against the gods, but when that failed, they were sent as Guardians to warn those who might be in danger," Jagger says, swirling the remaining liquid in his glass before drinking it back.

"They're usually only sent to warn travelers. So we're unsure on why one was sent to the school," Hunter adds.

"Do you think it has anything to do with getting your gifts back and The Elders?" Arlo asks, looking between all of us.

"There's been nothing so far to indicate that they even know about it. We don't even know if it's permanent or just temporary," I say, mostly to play devil's advocate.

It's been four months since Kane started gaining the ability to use his without The Elders relinquishing control of it to him, and so far it hasn't seemed to dimmed or disappear. In fact, the more time he spends around Arlo, the stronger he becomes. The stronger we all become. I feel almost like I did before we were sent to Earth. However, there's something preventing the curse from being fully broken. The possibility of getting back to being as strong as we once were is… well, I'm trying not to think about it too much in case things don't work out that way.

"But those other things," Arlo starts, "the ghost things. If they do find out about me—"

"They won't," Hunter grunts. "As far as they know you were just some girl we were mildly obsessed with. They don't know how important you are to us or they wouldn't have let us leave the city."

"That's another thing. You said whatever was protecting me for most of my life disappeared the minute I stepped foot on campus. Why?"

"We think it has something to do with it being where we first appeared when we were sent to Earth. We're almost positive that the first group also first appeared on the same land." Hunter pauses and regards Arlo carefully. Like, he's trying to figure out how to phrase his next words. "Do you remember ever going to visit the campus with your dad when you were younger?"

Her eyes narrow in thought and her brows furrow in the center. How can anyone be so freaking adorable. "Not that I can remember. My mom recently told me that he always wanted to go to Queen's University. Although she could never understand why. He wanted her to attend with him."

The guys and I exchange a look. We need to figure out what was there before the university was built because for some reason, we all feel drawn to it and it's not just because that was where we were placed originally. There's something else there, and I have a feeling it might just be the missing piece we need to end this curse.

"Like, I was saying. The ghost things—"

"Dybbuks," Jagger helpfully adds.

Arlo shoots him what I would consider her version of a death glare, but it doesn't quite have the effect she wants when the corner of her lips twitch. "You done?"

"I'm sorry." Jagger places a hand over his chest and mock bows. "Continue."

Arlo snorts. "How can you tell if someone is possessed by one?"

"Well," I start, switching her foot for the other one. I got so absorbed into the conversation and my thoughts that I hadn't realized I'd been rubbing the same foot for the last twenty minutes. "Generally speaking, most normal human beings aren't going to try and kill you."

Kane groans dropping his forehead to Hunter's shoulder as Hunter gives me a look that's more like a death glare than the one Arlo turned on Jagger.

"Nice," Hunter scoffs.

"What? It's the truth."

"So, are they like zombies?" Arlo asks.

Jagger chuckles, curling an arm around her shoulders. "No. They're very unzombie-like. They not dead, remember? The bodies they possess are very much alive."

"What happens to the bodies after they're done their job?"

I look at Hunter who's looking out over the frozen lake. When he speaks, he sounds like it's miles away. "It depends on how strong they were before being possessed. For some it'll be just like waking up from a dream but only remembering bits and pieces of it. Others don't make it."

We're all quiet as we try to digest that information. The three of us knew there was a possibility that Hunter had come into contact with a Dybbuk. Whether in this life or a previous one, but none of us have been able to get him to elaborate.

"Wait, so the people who are strong enough, who are able to survive, if they kill someone while possess do they still get charged with murder?" Arlo's grey eyes widen in a mix of shock and horror.

"You have to remember, Little Lamb, that humans are naturally suspicious about the supernatural. As in, the majority don't believe in it. It doesn't matter if the person who was possessed doesn't remember committing the crime. Their picture and or their DNA was at the crime scene. All the evidence points to them. So unless they actually suffer from some kind of mental illness, the judge and jury aren't going to believe that they didn't do it."

"That's bullshit," Arlo spits out, pushing to her feet and making the water slosh out over the sides.

"We didn't say we agreed with it, Little Lamb," Jagger says taking hold of her wrist and pulling her down onto his lap. "But it's the sad reality."

"But they're just innocent people who were made to do something horrible."

"We know, Charlotte. It's something we struggle with too," I say, giving her a small smile in hopes of not bringing down her mood even more.

"Have you guys ever—"

"Hell no," Kane says before she can finish asking her question, but I think we all know where she was going. "We don't mess with that shit."

That seems to pacify her for now. Since we've been in here for longer than we planned, Jagger helps Arlo out of the hot tub and into the house to get showered and changed while Kane and Hunter help me close up the hot tub and gather all the clothes and glasses that were strewn about.

Once everyone is showered and Arlo is tucked into bed, the four of us conjugate in the kitchen.

"We need to figure out what was on that land before they built the school," Hunter says but I'm already nodding along and pulling out my phone.

"I was thinking the same thing earlier. Whatever was or is there could be the key in figuring out why the curse hasn't broken yet." I pull up google and begin a search for the history of the school.

"Have you talked to Hades yet?" Jagger asks, placing a steaming mug of hot tea in front of Hunter. We all know he won't be able to sleep if he doesn't drink caffeine before bed. Hunter's brain works a million miles a second, but somehow the caffeine seems to help settle him enough that he's able to fall asleep.

He glances out the window above the sink and then turns back to us. "Not yet. Supposed to meet him down by the lake at two."

"Want me to tag along?" I ask, bumping his shoulder with mine.

He returns the nudge but before he can respond there's a loud boom that sounds like gunshots or a car backfiring. The floor begins to shake. Picture frames and artwork on the wall crash to the floor. Candle holders and decorations that were on top of shelves topple over and crash to the hardwood floor.

Kane and I turn wide eyes on each other then we're both scrambling to get to Arlo while trying to avoid by other household items. Just as we get to the bedroom door and fling it open, the shaking stops.

Arlo sits with her back against the headboard, her knees drawn up to her chest and her arms curled over her head.

"C'mon, Little Lamb," Kane coaxes. "Let's go."

I search the room for clothes for her to throw on but the only ones I can see are a pair of black sweat pants that are probably Hunter's and a Queen's University football sweater that most likely belongs to Jagger. I gather them up and hand them to Arlo. I leave Kane to help her get dressed and go in search of the other guys.

"What the hell was that?" I ask, finding them staring out the window of the living room.

Jagger turns terrified eyes on me. I don't think I've ever seen him this scared in the hundreds of years I've known him. "They know."

CHAPTER THIRTEEN

HUNTER

"**T**HEY KNOW."

Two words I knew would come eventually but was hoping would come only minutes or seconds before the curse was broken. Now, as I stand staring at the three Elders while surrounded by the four people I would die for, I know that was a stupid, naive hope. I glance back over my shoulder towards the back door, not surprised in the least to not see Hades. It's only a little after midnight, the man's never been early for anything.

"What does that mean? What do we do now?" Arlo asks, taking a step towards the window but I stop her with an arm across her chest and pull her back.

"I'm going out there to talk to them. You all stay here." I look to Wolf. Out of the three of them, he'll be able to resist Arlo's pleas the longest. Not by much, none of us are that strong or heartless, but enough that I can convince them to leave and come back another time. "Don't let her get close to that window." I don't say much else but the words I left unspoken are clear. They're not going to take lightly to what we did.

Thankfully, he doesn't argue. Just grunts and pulls Arlo out of my arms and into his. I lean down to press a kiss to the top of her head then slip out of the hold she still has on the sleeve of my shirt.

"Hunter," she calls as I'm reaching for the handle on the front door. "Be safe."

I try to swallow passed the dryness in my throat and give her a clipped nod. I don't have the words to give her. Not the ones she wants to hear anyway. I can't guarantee my safety out here. They're too unpredictable. Despite the shit I've done in my life, I've always kept my promises. *Always.* To protect the people inside this cabin, I have to be willing to do whatever it takes. Even if it means not stepping foot back inside the house. Even if it means not getting to feel Arlo and the other guys in my arms one last time.

"James," I greet the man in the front. "Sean. Randall." I nod at the others. Hoping my voice comes out as cool and collected as I'm trying to appear. "I'm surprised to see you out here." *Especially since this is technically holy grounds with it being owned by Tron.*

Sean begins to step forward, but James stops him with a hand held up before he steps forward. His immaculate dress shoes crunching in the snow with every step. He stops a couple feet away and doesn't attempt to get closer.

"We heard a rumour and we were hoping you'd be able to put it to rest for us," he says, his slight Middle Eastern accent coating his words.

"And what rumour would that be?"

"That the girl has somehow granted you temporary use of your powers."

Temporary?

I frown, but quickly cover it up with a chuckle. "I would think that you would know if we were granted any of our powers back. After all, you were the ones who created this curse."

Sean purses his lips and curls his hands into fists at his side. It doesn't take a genius to know that if James wasn't here, Sean would've liked nothing more than to hit me. Randall, stoic as ever, just watches the exchange in front of him. Some days, I wonder what it would be like to see inside his mind. Then again, maybe I'm glad I can't.

"Hmm," James hums. "If that's the case then maybe we should confirm it, shouldn't we?"

I brace myself as James gets closer and reaches out a hand toward me. The last time this happened, we all had to watch helplessly as Wolf crumbled to his knees. I'm aware that even with bracing myself for what I know is coming, it won't make it any less painful. I don't know what's worse; knowing you're about to die or having your gift of death used against you. James plants a hand on my shoulder. I flinch automatically in response to the pain about to wrack my body, but nothing comes. He shares my look of shock as he squeezes my shoulder. Nothing. I take the opportunity to step out of his hold, careful not to let the other two out of my sights. I'm also hyper-aware of my surroundings. These fuckers could have anyone or any-thing hiding in plain sight.

James twists around and stalks back to the other two Elders. While their heads are bent together and they seem to be distracted, I decide to use this time to see if the guys have any answers on what just happened.

Me: What the fuck just happened?

Jagger: Um, well... I think...

Wolf: I'm not 100% sure, but...

Kane: Huh

Me: Somebody spit it out.

Kane: I think we figured out Arlo's role in all this.

Me: The fuck is that supposed to mean?

Arlo: I can hear you!

Jagger: Remember how we couldn't figure out why whatever was protecting her suddenly disappeared?

Me: Yeah.

Jagger: Well, we figured it out. At least Hades thinks we have.

Me: Hades?

Movement out of the corner of my eye catches my attention. My devil of an ex, leans against the trunk of a tree, his ankles crossed over each other and hands stuffed in the front pockets of a pair of black dress pants. The one time he decides to show up early just *had* to be today.

Without another word, the trio in front of me disappear. Just *poof.* Vanishing without the same dramatics as when they appeared. That makes me even more worried. What the fuck were they discussing that had them just taking off without another word. I slump against the side of the cabin and rub my forehead, hoping that a full-blown migraine isn't in my immediate future.

"Looks like you got yourself into some predicament, H," Hades says, joining me in front of the house. He flicks the butt of his cigarette into the snow and then toes it out.

"Nice of you to join us," I grumble, turning and heading for the front door.

As soon as I clear the threshold, Arlo flings herself into my arms and I barely manage to catch her while staying upright.

"Don't ever do something so stupid again," she berates, while burying her nose in the crook of my neck and holding me tight. "The guys told me what happened the last time they used your powers against you. I remember what it felt like too," she adds in a small voice.

I tighten my hold around her waist and lift her up. She wraps her legs around my waist and I carry her into the living room, not letting go when I take a seat on the sofa. I don't apologize to her even though that's what I know she wants. I've always prided myself on being a man of my word, no matter what life has dealt us. Plus, I just can't lie to her because I'm not sorry. I'd be the one to go out there again in a heartbeat if I need to. I would rather it be me than have to stay back inside the house and watch any one of these four suffer out there alone.

"Well, this isn't what I had in mind when you said you wanted to see me," Hades comments, leaning a shoulder against the wall that separates the living room from the entranceway, just like he was doing outside.

"And what did you think I meant?" I ask, over Arlo's shoulder.

Hades grins, suggestively. "That you missed me. Maybe that you were tired of these three already and wanted another wild night."

Arlo's back vibrates under my palms and it takes me a minute to realize that she's growling. It sounds like a wild baby wolf, but it's definitely a growl.

"Settle down there, cub. I'm joking. Mostly," he says to her, but the glare she turns on him would be enough to bring a normal mortal to their knees. If Hades was mortal and you know, normal.

"Jagger said you figured out why James couldn't hurt me out there," I say, trying to steer the topic into safer territory.

Hades playfulness is immediately replaced by a serious expression I have only seen on him twice since I've known him. Once when I asked him to keep Chaos leashed for me and once when he found out that the three of us were being sent to Earth. He wasn't happy. In fact, he was the opposite of happy. He didn't want me to do it. If I remember correctly, he even called it the worst mistake I could ever make. I had hoped he'd tell me it was because he wanted us to be together and me being sent to Earth would make that impossible, but that wasn't the case. It was his pure hatred for humanity that was the driving force behind his need to keep me from agreeing to come. Like, I ever had a choice in the matter, though.

"Have you ever heard of the power of causality manipulation?"

Arlo twists around in my lap so she's sitting across me with her feet on the other side of the couch and her head on my shoulder. I look at the other guys but they're all shaking their head.

"It's one of the gifts that were eradicated at the turn of the sixteenth century," I say, confused on what this has to do with anything.

"We all thought it was eradicated. There's been no mention of anyone, supernatural or not, with the gift." He pauses, then looks at Arlo curled up in my arms. "Until now."

"What are you saying?" Jagger asks at the same time Arlo says, "What? I have no gifts. I can't even boil water without it burning."

"Causality Manipulation is the ability to bend cause and effect to one's will. At one point in time it was said to protect the user more than just a protection shield since they could control what happens to them and those around them. However, some thought it made them more powerful than everyone else and used it for evil, for lack of a better word. Those were often imprisoned and executed, except for one. He somehow managed to elude being captured and was only discovered when he was on his deathbed, but by that time it was too late. Who knows how many children he had fathered after he disappeared. And when the gift never materialized again after that, it was assumed that it had ended with him." Hades pushes off the wall to take a seat beside Kane on the love-seat.

He rubs his palms down the thighs of his pants and leans forward to rest his elbows on his knees, with his hands clasped together. His blond hair falls in his eyes and my fingers still twitch with the memory of all the times I used to comb it back. There's no emotional connection between us anymore, but that doesn't mean that the memories are gone.

"But I thought you were immortal? How could he have been on his deathbed?" Arlo asks.

"We are, but no one is truly safe from death." Hades glances at me and smirks before continuing his explanation. It's one the rest of us have heard before. "We all have that one thing that could be our down-fall. Vampires have the sun. Werewolves have silver and wolfsbane. We have..." he glances at me and I subtly shake my head. She doesn't need to know that right now. "Well, that's for these guys to tell you. My point is, I think the gift was just dormant for all those years."

Silence descends around us at Hades' words until Wolf shuffles his weight from one foot to the other where he's standing beside the fireplace. His pant legs rustling against each other. "Who was the guy?"

"Paul Williams. Father to Joseph Williams."

Andréa Joy

"MY GRANDFATHER?" My voice comes out as little more than a whisper.

Hades goes on to explain that my grandfather had an affair with a mortal woman on one of his trips to Earth. Paul didn't know that she had had a baby until he fled here to avoid capture. My grandparents raised my dad without any knowledge of his heritage.

"In fact, I don't think your grandfather ever told your grandmother the truth about what he was. Your dad didn't find out the truth until after your grandfather died. Once he was discovered, he was recruited as part of the Four Horsemen because as evil as Paul was before he fled, he was also arguably one of the more powerful Guardians. We think that's what drove a wrench between your dad and the other three horsemen. That and the fact that he fell in love with a mortal human just like his father did. No one knows how Paul went undetected all those years, but my guess is Witches."

I lean forward on Hunter's lap and blink at Hades. My head begins to ache with the forming of an impending headache. Hunter's warm palms gently caresses circles onto my back, and as much as I wish I could relax into his touch, I can't.

"Did they kill him?" I ask Hades. Both needing to know and dreading the answer. My entire life there was this thought festering at the back of my mind that my dad's death wasn't what people were telling me. My mom was too tight lipped about the death of the man she loved. While I never expected her to talk about his death, I found it odd that she just wouldn't talk about him at all. Not even the good times they had together. If it were me, I'd want to make sure that my daughter knew everything there was to know about her dad.

Hades eyes bounce from Kane beside him to Wolf to Jagger and then Hunter before finally landing back on me. But when they do, I know I have his full attention. "I believe they tried, yes."

My head is pounding now. I need just a minute to process everything that's been told to me over the last several months. I climb off Hunter's lap and hold out a hand when my four guys start to follow me. "I just need a minute," I say, and then head down the hallway to close myself off in one of the bedrooms.

Angels. Devils. Magical Beings. Mythical Creatures. If someone had told me six months ago that this would be my life, I would've laughed in their face. Like, full out belly laughed. And then I would've told them to go smoke another joint. This is just crazy. What's even more messed up is the fact that my family seemed to be right in the middle of it, and yet I had no idea until just a few minutes ago. Did my mom know? And if she did then why was she keeping it from me all these years? Didn't she think I had a right to know about my heritage?

Tired of all the unanswered questions swirling around my head, I pull my phone from my back pocket and sit on the foot of the double bed. It rings a few times before my mom's voice comes through the other side of the phone.

"Hi honey, I wasn't expecting to hear from you today. Is everything okay?"

I suck in a deep breath before asking, "What was my grandfather like?"

Mom laughs lightly on the other end of the line. "Arlo, you know your grandfather."

"No," I say, cutting her off before she can say more. "I meant dad's father. Paul." The line goes silent for so long, I pull the phone away from my ear to check to see that the call wasn't dropped. It wasn't. "Mom."

"Where did you hear that name?"

The change in her voice tells me all I need to know. She knew.

"Is it all true? My dad…." I have to pause to take a breath. "My dad was half–"

"How did you find this out? Where are you?" She sounds frantic now. I hear muffled voices in the background as she talks to someone. "Arlo, honey, where are you? I'm coming to get you so we can talk."

"No," I say forcefully. Almost too forcefully when the door to the bedroom flies open and four angry and concerned men fill the doorway. I wince and mouth, "sorry," to them before continuing to talk to my mom. "I just… why didn't you tell me?" I swallow down a sob and then another when Kane comes over and pulls me into his arms.

She huffs. "There really was no need to, Charlotte." I flinch at the use of my full name. She never calls me Charlotte unless she's mad at me or she's disappointed. "As soon as we found out about you, your dad walked away from that life. He chose us. Why would I tell you about something that has no impact on your life?"

Except it does, I think to myself.

"Just a minute, babe. I'm on the phone with Arlo," she says to someone in the background. To me she says, "Look, I don't know what brought this up but you need to come home so we can talk about it. Adrian is leaving in a few hours, why don't you come by and have dinner?"

Kane stiffens behind me, obviously having heard both sides of the conversation. "She can't trust Adrian, Little Lamb.

His real name is Randall," Kane whispers into my other ear.

I whip my head around at that name while goosebumps pebble up my arms. Why does that name sound familiar?

"Sorry, mom," I say, even though I don't feel sorry at all. How could she have thought this wasn't important enough to tell me. "Maybe some other time." I hang up in the midst of her trying to tell me to wait.

I step out of Kane's embrace and throw my phone on the duvet before turning around to face my men, and Hades. "Who's Randall?"

Hades chuckles, leaning a shoulder against the wall and eating a bag of popcorn. Can this man never stand up straight when there's a wall around? He looks like the TV version of Lucifer, just blond and green-eyed, and more muscular. And is that a tattoo on his neck? I shake myself out of whatever stupor I was in and look to the other guys.

"He's one of the Elders. James is the oldest. Sean is the hot-headed one and the youngest, and Randall is the unpredictable one. His face always looks like it's set in stone," Jagger explains.

"The man never gives anything away and it's impossible to figure him out," Kane adds.

"Why is he pretending to be your dad? And why didn't you tell me?" I ask Hunter, my hands curling into fists at my side. I'm sick and tired of being the last one to find out shit.

"That night we had dinner at your house, I didn't know that's where we were going. I was as shocked as you were when you opened that door. After Halloween, they found out that we weren't exactly being truthful about who you were to us," Hunter says.

Before he can go on, Wolf buts in. "We tried playing it off like you meant nothing to us in hopes that it would protect you by drawing their attention off you."

"Obviously it didn't work. After they found out that we had lied, we were tortured for months. James knows exactly how to kill us, but he doesn't have the means to. Instead, he got off on bringing us to the brink. So much so, that there were a couple days that we begged for him to just end it."

Movement across the room draws my attention and I see Jagger pulling Kane into his side and kissing the side of his head. For someone who wields the power of war, he's the most emotional one of the group. Hades still looks disinterested in the whole conversation, but I can see the interest he tries to hide in his eyes.

"Anyway, after those couple months, they finally let us go on one condition that I accompany Randall to a dinner. They didn't say much more and I wasn't about to question it if it meant we got out of that basement." Hunter pauses again, this time to reach over and take my hand in his. "I didn't understand their reasoning behind that dinner, but now I do."

"And what's that?" I croak.

"They wanted to show them that they could get to you. Always. That no matter what they did to protect you, you weren't safe," Hades adds.

Hunter nods, solemnly. "It was a warning to the four of us. We should've just stayed away from you after that, but then I saw you on campus and I knew I could never do that."

"For the record," Jagger says, "Neither of us could. Stay away from you that is. When Hunter told us that he saw you that night, we were ready to march to your house and demand you talk to us."

I smile despite the tears threatening to spill down my cheeks. "As mad as I was at all of you, I think I would've seen you. Those few months away from you were the hardest I've ever had to go through, and I could never understand why." I look up at Hunter and run the back of a finger down his scruffy jaw. My eyes track to Wolf standing slightly in front of but beside Hades and then over to Kane and

Jagger. "It's because I'm one of you, isn't it? This bond isn't just because I lo-like you all." I internally kick myself for almost confessing that what I feel for them is so much more than like.

"Like I was saying earlier," Hades jumps in, licking his fingers of the butter from the popcorn. "You, my dear, have the gift of causality manipulation." He tosses the popcorn bag in the trash in the corner of the room and then rubs his hands together with a gleeful smile. "I can't wait to see the looks on the faces of those three when they find out they're not the big bad anymore. I've been waiting centuries for them to get theirs after what they did to you four."

Confused, I look back to Hunter. He sighs and rubs his forehead. "The Elders were the Four Horsemen before we were tasked with the job. Until your dad met and fell in love with your mom. We were never meant to fall in love with different people. Our powers are the strongest when we're together. We were always meant to stick together as a four and add a fifth. Your dad picked love over duty and as a result they all lost their gifts and standings as Guardians. They can never go back to where we came from."

"But if they aren't magical anymore then how were they able to curse you?"

"Witches. All three of them wear a talisman around their neck. It gives them the ability to cast curses and communicate with demons," Wolf adds.

We all look at Hades.

"Hey. Woah, don't give me those looks. I don't deal in demons. Those fuckers are just spirits who've gotten trapped and are in limbo. I have nothing to do with them."

"That's some *Princess and the Frog* type bullshit," I mutter under my breath which earns a round of chuckles from the guys.

"She's not wrong," Hades agrees. "Well, as fun as it's been, duty calls." He knocks the door frame a couple times when he turns to go but then stops and looks back at Hunter over his shoulder.

"I'll leave Ceb here for a few days. If the Elders do plant anything in the surrounding woods, he'll be able to sniff them out before they get too close. You have ten more days before Chaos breaks free. I suggest you use them wisely," he says and then he's gone. A few seconds later, the back-door slams shut followed by a howl so chilling, I scoot closer to Hunter until he wraps an arm around my shoulders.

"Tell me he wasn't talking about the three-headed dog," I plead, looking up at Hunter who has the audacity to just grin. "Fucking hell."

Wolf laughs, "Don't worry, Little Lamb. He's not much of a people person. The mutt will probably just roam the land until Hades calls him back." And then he too is walking out of the room. We hear the back door open and close again, followed by, "Who's a good boy." And what I assume would be a playful yip coming from any other normal dog but sounds anything but coming from the devil dog.

"Do you want to go say hi," Jagger suggests, but I'm already shaking my head.

"Nope. No. Hell no. Hell to the no." I stop and tilt my head. "I wonder how many ways there are to say no." To Jagger I say, "I've seen pictures of what people think that beast looks like. I don't want more nightmares, thank you very much."

Kane laughs, taking my hand and pulling me up off the bed. "He's not that scary. He's actually a big teddy bear."

"Until he accidentally bites off a limb," I mumble under my breath which causes the guys to laugh.

When Wolf comes back from a run with the devil dog, I make him go take a shower before he climbs into bed with Kane and me. We figured out real fast that the five of us weren't going to fit on the queen-sized mattress. So, two of them will rotate sleeping in the bed with me while the other two sleep on the pull-out couch on the other side of the room. After the day I've had, it doesn't take long before

I'm falling asleep cocooned in Kane and Wolf's arms.

Andréa Joy

KANE

"I FIGURED IT OUT," I say, excitedly, while dancing in my seat. It took a lot of researching and googling but I finally figured out the answer.

"Figured what out?" Jagger says, scratching his belly while he pours fresh coffee in his mug.

My jaw drops as I watch his fingers move over smooth skin. I lick my lips as I think about the way he shivered under my mouth as I kissed him there and then again when I kissed the spot right below his belly button in the shower this morning while the others slept.

"Kane," he growls, sexily, making my dick stand up and take notice.

"Hm?"

Wolf laughs, bumping his shoulder into mine. "Someone needs a good pound-ing." In my ear he whispers, "Is someone feeling left out?"

I sigh, while it's true that since Arlo has become a more permanent addition to our group I haven't been dicked as much as before, I still can't complain. Although, it would be nice to be pushed over a counter or table from time to time and fucked until I can't stand anymore.

Jagger grins as he joins Wolf and I at the table. "I take that dopey smile as a yes."

I shrug, focusing on my phone and hoping that the heat spreading across my face isn't all that obvious. "A guy has needs," I mutter under my breath and then change the subject back to my findings. "I figured out what the land the school is built on was used as before."

"And what's that?" Hunter asks, as he and Arlo join us in the kitchen, looking freshly showered, and by the flush of Arlo's cheeks, freshly fucked too.

"A cemetery."

Jagger sputters and chokes on his coffee, spewing liquid everywhere. "Sorry," he grunts, reaching for the paper towel holder so he can clean up his mess.

"Run that by us again," Wolf says.

"A cemetery. And guess who was buried there."

"Paul Williams," Hunter guesses correctly.

At Arlo's confused look, I go on to explain what I found. "Paul died in the eighteen century, but because there was no record of him technically being born, there's obviously no record of him having died. I had to comb through tons and tons of articles until I found the right one. Really, it was just a picture of the cemetery with a bunch of tombstones in the background but I was able to zoom in a bit on one in the very back." I find the picture I'm talking about and zoom in before turning my phone around and handing it to Jagger. "It doesn't have his years of birth and death, but it does have the–"

"Crossed Spears," Hunter says, looking over Jagger's shoulders.

"Okay, and?" Arlo frowns, taking the phone from Jagger when he hands it to her.

"The Crossed Spears have double meanings. In the ancient times here on Earth, it was used as a symbol of protection. However, in a witches hands it was a symbol of disagreement. Where we're from, the Crossed Spears is a symbol of the Guardians."

"So you think that the reason why my dad and I feel so drawn to that school is because that's where my grandfather is buried?"

I nod. "I believe so, yes. You and your dad aren't the only ones who feel a draw to that place. The four of us do too, and I believe the four before us did as well, but I think that had more to do with your dad being part of them than any of them feeling an actual draw." I inhale a deep breath before putting the rest of my thoughts out there. "I also believe that that's where we'll have the most luck in fully breaking the curse."

Wolf's spoon clinks as he drops it in his bowl of cereal. "That puts us in the open for The Elders to use the Dybbuks and any other demon creature they can conjure."

"But I think we'll also be more powerful. Plus, if Hades is right and Arlo has the gift of causality manipulation then we can use that to our advantage. Actually, I thought a lot about that and it makes sense. Neither one of us could sense her until she stepped foot on that campus. I think that's because some part of you knew," I say, turning to Arlo.

"Are you saying it was fate?"

"Maybe or maybe not. But I don't think it's a coincidence that not even six months before you came to campus, the four of us decided that we were ready to settle down and find the fifth to complete our bond. It explains your undeniable draw to the school."

"But it doesn't explain how whatever protection was surrounding her disappeared," Wolf says.

"Actually," I stop pacing and lean back against the half counter that separates the kitchen from the dining room. "It does. I don't think Joseph did cast any sort of protection spell over her." Addressing Arlo directly, I say, "Whether you were aware of it or not, I think your subconscious must have known that you were in danger after your dad left and in order to protect yourself, you unknowingly drew on the power passed down from your grandfather. Your subconscious probably felt safe enough when you were on campus to withdraw the shield."

When I'm done talking, there are four sets of eyes staring oddly at me with mouths agape. "What?"

Jagger exhales a fast breath and runs his hand through his hair. "How the hell did you come up with all of that overnight while the rest of us were sleeping?"

I shrug. "My power is war which means I'm use to analyzing battle plans and seeing the smaller details. I wasn't sure if any of it would make sense. And then I saw that picture and the pieces started fitting together. Especially after what Hades told us last night."

Arlo's suspiciously quiet as she goes about getting down a glass and filling it with ice and water before coming to stand beside me. "I don't feel very powerful." She pouts. "None of that explains why my dad attacked me all those months ago," she says, folding an arm across her middle.

"It kinda does," Jagger says, getting up to join us. "If Joseph thought that we were anything like those other three and he knew his baby girl was getting involved with us, he would do everything he could to warn her away."

"You guys are nothing like those jerks," Arlo declares.

"No, we're not," I agree, putting an arm around her. "But he doesn't know that. Frankly, I don't blame him. He doesn't see Hunter, Wolf, Jagger, or Kane. He only sees War, Famine, Plague, and Death, and he only knows what he did with the other three when they were the Horsemen. And what they tried doing to him when he walked away."

The tension leaves her shoulders as she relaxes into my side. I kiss the top of her head and slip her glass out of her fingers with my free hand, placing it on the counter behind us.

"So, what now?"

"Now, you go snowmobiling with Wolf and Jagger while Hunter and I go to the school."

Several minutes later, Hunter and I are piling into his SUV while Jagger pulls open the garage door where the snowmobiles are kept. We're about half-way back to Toronto when I can't keep my anxiety quiet anymore. My leg starts bouncing, my fingers tapping out a random rhythm on the inside door rest.

"Do you think this all seems too easy?" I ask Hunter, chewing on my bottom lip.

He glances at me out of the corner of his eye as he flips on his right signal to switch lanes. "Easy is good. We could use easy right now. Though, I'm still not sure what we need to do after we get there. The curse isn't going to magically break. It hasn't before when we've all been on campus at the same time."

"Yeaaah," I say, drawing out the word. "I think we might have to contact Joseph and ask for his help."

Hunter snorts, directing the vehicle off the highway. "Good luck with that. He's not going to want to talk to us, and even if he does, Arlo might not be ready for that."

"We'll have to try. He could be the only one who knows exactly what the others did to cast it and therefore might be the only one outside of the Elders who knows how to undo it."

He hums but doesn't respond and just continues driving until we pull into the far parking lot of the university by the football fields and the gym. We both hop out and I pull up the picture on my phone again to see if I can find any landmarks that might still be the same.

Tucked between the gym and the science building is the same Angel statute as the picture. It's been restored over the years but the wings in mid-flight and hand reaching toward the sky are the same.

"Do you feel any different?" I ask Hunter, even as I look around the immediate area. I'm not even sure what I'm looking for. The tombstones were removed to make room for the buildings and the field. The only sign that this used to be a cemetery is the Angel we're standing in front of.

Hunter shakes his head, sliding his hand into the front pockets of his black jeans and looks around too. "Are we sup-posed to feel something? Like a power surge?" He grins playfully.

My shoulders drop in defeat. If I'm wrong about this then it's reasonable to believe that I'm wrong about everything.

"Hey," Hunter says, sensing my mood. He throws an arm around my shoulders and pulls me into his side. "It's okay. We'll figure out another way. We have time."

"Nine days isn't a long time." I pull out of his embrace and walk around the statue, trying to look for any clues that either proves me right or wrong. Either way, I need a solid sign. As if my thoughts are being answered, my gaze gets snagged on something etched into the stone. If I hadn't been looking for something that looks like it didn't quite fit, I wouldn't have seen it. But there in amongst the natural wear and tear of the statue from the years and changing of seasons, is the markings of the Crossed Spear. The same one that was on Paul Williams' tombstone.

"Hunter," I breathe, searching for his hand without taking my eyes off the symbol.

"What is it?"

He slides his palm against mine and I pull him closer, reaching our joined hands out to trace along the edges of the symbol.

"Holy shit. Is that?"

I grin. "It is."

A throat clears behind us and we both turn to find an oddly familiar man watching us. His baseball hat is pulled down to conceal his eyes and he's dressed in white-washed jeans and a sky-blue Henley underneath a leather jacket, but it's his presence that feels familiar.

"Can we help you?" Hunter asks, turning around to face the newcomer and subtly moving to shield me with his body. I huff in frustration at the move, but don't try to push him back.

"Stay away from my daughter."

He tips the bill of his hat up and it's then I get a glimpse of eyes the same shade of grey as Arlo's.

"We're not the ones trying to hurt her. We're trying to protect her." I place a hand on Hunter's bicep and try to get him to move over but he doesn't budge. I roll my eyes and take a step to the side and forward, putting me equal with him. He scowls at me over his shoulder and I return it with an innocent grin. I have been known to send grown men cowering, but yet the guys still treat me like I'm the more fragile one of the group.

Joseph snickers and gets right up into my face. Hunter stiffens beside me but thankfully doesn't intervene. "If that were true you would've left her alone the minute you found out who she was."

Hunter snorts, drawing Joseph's attention. "Clearly you don't know your daughter very well. She's stubborn than all get out and more curious than a puppy who's been given a new toy."

I bite down on my lip to keep from laughing. If Arlo were to hear Hunter compare her to a puppy, I'm not sure if she would kick his ass because he compared to her a dog or swoon because he thinks her that cute.

"What's that supposed to mean?"

"It means, Arlo was going to do whatever she wanted, whether we tried to keep our distance or not. But you and I both know that that's impossible in the world we live in. She was going to find out the truth sooner or later. I'm just glad that we were there to guide her when she did instead of her having to go about it alone because you abandoned her," I say, pressing a finger into his chest and getting into his face just like he did to me.

"Kane," Hunter warns, but I'm already on a roll.

"If you hadn't taken the cowards way out and disappeared when you did, she could've had you to teach her about our life and who she is."

"You better watch what you say to me. You have no idea the reasons I did what I did," Joseph seethes, pushing closer.

"Or what? You gonna attack her again to warn her away? Or put another note in her locker?" I scoff, removing my finger from his chest and folding my arms across mine. "You would've had a better chance if you told her the truth about who you are. Instead, you did the opposite of what you wanted. You drove her further into our arms."

"Trust me," he says, taking a step back and sliding his hands into the pockets of his jeans as he watches students walk across the lightly snow-covered field on their way to class. "I'm well aware of that fact."

Hunter sighs, bracing his hands on his hips as he regards both Joseph and me. Finally, he says, "we're not like your harem, Joseph. We're not as vindictive and conniving as James and Sean."

He shakes his head and pinches the bridge of his nose between his thumb and forefinger. "Maybe, but you're underestimating Randall. Don't think that just because he takes on a more observational role when they appear to you that it doesn't mean he's not just as vindictive." He drops his hand and his eyes plead with us to understand and take his next words seriously. "Don't ever turn your back on him. It's the quiet ones who won't think twice before plunging a knife into your back."

Hunter and I glance at each other. We always thought that it was James behind the threats and manipulation, but what if it were really Randall, and James was just the voice. Hunter's the first one to break our stare off.

"Why don't you come back with us? Arlo will probably love to see you."

I frown and shoot him a glare. What happened to, *"it's too soon. She's probably not ready."* Hunter's lips subtly twitch as he tries not to smile. Alright, Hunter Anderson, I see what you did there.

With a little more nudging, Joseph agrees to come back to the cabin in Utterson with us. We make the trip north without any snack breaks this time since we left Jagger behind, and get back to the cabin in just over two hours.

CHAPTER SIXTEEN

JAGGER

I MANAGE TO GET the snowmobiles gassed up and ready to go not long after Kane and Hunter disappear down the driveway and head back to the city. Arlo and Wolf join me out in the garage a few minutes later and Arlo hops on the front of my snowmobile while Wolf takes the other one. I scoot forward until there's nothing separating our bodies except for the layers of clothes to protect us against the cold wind and snow and press the inside of my thighs against hers. I gave her a quick crash course in how to steer and operate the vehicle and then we're on our way to one of the many trails surrounding the cabin with Wolf following at a good distance behind us.

"There should be a small ice rink down here," I lean in to say close to her ear and tap her left hand to indicate that she should turn left at the parting in the trees.

Arlo nods and maneuvers the snowmobile down the narrower trail until the rink comes into view just a little ways up ahead. As soon as we're stopped and she has the vehicle turned off, I hop off and offer her a gloved hand which she takes with a, "thank you."

"If I knew were heading down here I would've brought some skates," Wolf says coming to stop beside our snowmobile and joining us at the rink.

I shrug. "Our boots should be fine." I had checked the tread on them earlier before going out to get the snowmobiles ready and noticed that neither of them had the greatest tread, which would normally piss me off since having good tread on your boots while up here could mean the difference between a small injury and a bigger one, but for right now they'll come in handy.

Taking Arlo's hand in mine, I tug her along with me and step onto the iced surface. "Did you ever think you'd be skating on a piece of the Canadian Shield?"

Her laugh is light. Happy in the quiet mid-morning light as she throws her head back. "Can't say I have."

Wolf takes her other hand, and together the three of us skate loops around the makeshift rink. The only thing we're missing is a holiday playlist and some hot chocolate to make this day even more perfect. When Arlo starts to shiver against the wind that's begun picking up, we head back to the snowmobiles. This time she rides back with Wolf and I follow behind them. As soon as we re-enter the house, Wolf bends to hook a shoulder into her stomach and throws her over in a fireman's carry, slapping her ass on the way to a hot shower. After making sure the cabin is secure and Ceb hasn't picked up on any trespassers, I start shucking clothes on my way to join Wolf and Arlo in the shower.

Quiet moans greet my ears before I even have the door pushed open. The glass of the shower door is already steamed up, except for a small area where there's a hand pressing against the glass. I pull open the door and step inside the six-person shower with double shower heads on one wall as well as a rain shower head above. Wolf has Arlo pressed against the opposite wall and he's on his knees, with one of her legs thrown over his shoulder. Her head is tilted back as she moans and her fingers tighten into the hair at his scalp. Now that I'm beginning to warm up, my cock begins filling with blood at the sight in front of me. I lick my lips and slide in beside her, tweaking one of her nipples between my fingers. Her hips buck and Wolf groans around her clit.

After a few more licks, he drops her foot back to the shower floor and stands to his full height, curling a hand around my neck and pulling me into a kiss, forcing me to taste her on his tongue. I groan into his mouth and try to deepen the kiss but he pulls away before I have a chance to.

"I want to watch you fuck her. Just like before." His eyes darken at the memory of that night in my room months ago. "And this time, I'm going to touch. I'm going to fuck that tight hole while you're inside of her."

Arlo's little whimper draws both our attention and we look down to see her hand disappearing between her thighs while her other one cups a breast.

Wolf tsks, gripping the wrist of the hand between her thighs. "That's ours, Little Lamb."

Feeling like I'm already on the brink and ready to explode, I grab a handful of the hair at the back of her head and yank her face to mine. I lick along her top lip and nip at the flesh of her plump bottom one. She gasps and opens for me, letting my tongue explore her mouth. When I can't hold back anymore, I let go of her hair and grip her hips, spinning her round to face the wall. Her hands shoot out to brace against the slippery tile and I reach down to place my cock at her entrance.

When I feel Wolf's tongue lick round my ass hole, I push forward. Arlo's breath hitches when I first enter her but then she sighs like she knows this is where I belong. I reach around her and play with her clit while Wolf gets me ready for his cock. Soon we're all connected. When Wolf thrusts forward so do I. It doesn't take either of us long to come like this. Arlo comes first which triggers my own release and then Wolf comes with a roar before biting down on my shoulder and filling my hole with his cum.

Wolf and I each take turns, washing Arlo. He takes his time running the soapy sponge all over her worn out body while I wash her hair. When her eyes begin to droop close, I lift her in my arms and carry her out of the shower and sit her on the counter so I can dry her off while Wolf rummages around for something for her to wear. He comes back with an old t-shirt of Hunter's and I slip it over her head and help her thread her arms through. When she's dressed, Wolf lifts her up and carries her to the bed.

"You're not joining me?" She mumbles sleepily.

"We will in a little while," I say, planting a kiss on her forehead and covering her with the duvet cover. Slipping his hand in mine, Wolf leads us out of the room, making sure to close the door as quietly as possible and together we head out to the living room.

"Did he say how far out they were?"

"No," he shakes his head, pulling out his phone to re-read the message Hunter sent us as we arrived back at the house. "I'm guessing not long now."

I blow out a breath and drop down on the biggest sofa. "I don't know how well she's going to take it."

"Well," he says, sitting down next to me before laying down with his head in my lap. I gently comb my fingers through his hair, scratching his scalp with my nails every so often. "I guess we're about to find out."

ARLO

A Week Later...

I'M STILL NOT entirely sure how I feel about my father being back, but I can't say that I'm exactly mad about it. Oh, I was at first when Hunter and Kane showed up with him five days ago, but I've had sufficient time to come to terms with him being back. Plus, the things he's been teaching me have been invaluable. My men agree with me too. My dad has been able to answer a lot of the questions they've had about what exactly happened before he disappeared.

"By the time I met your mom, Randall and James were already actively working to find loopholes so they could use our powers to bring about their own apocalypse. I think they already sensed early on that I was opposed to their idea. We were sent to patrol the Earth, not cause any more harm to it. So, they stopped talking about it whenever I was around and started sneaking off behind my back. We'd lost everything we'd built our relationship on by then, but I still missed the companionship, the intimacy. That's why I don't think it was all too hard to fall in love with your mom." He smiles, but his eyes glaze over like he's some place far away from here. "You could just tell, that when you talked, she gave you her full attention. I always got flack for looking older than what I said I was, but James was the one who decided we should start our journey on Earth as high school students." My dad rolls his eyes at the memory and scoffs. "The only good thing that came out of that was giving me the chance to meet your mom, and you."

"What happened when you found out she was pregnant?" I ask, curling my hands tighter around the mug of peppermint tea Kane brought me earlier.

"I suspect that those three knew about my relationship with your mom all along. We never did try to hide it, but we didn't flaunt it in front of them either. The last straw came when they found out she was pregnant. I already had one foot out at that point so it was a no-brainer to me to pick your mother. Randall was furious. I don't think James and Sean cared as much since we were never that close."

I finger the string of the teabag and swirl it around the now cold water. "Were you ever in the Navy?"

"I really was. Everything you remember from your childhood is the truth." He starts to reach over to cover my hand with his but thinks better of it and pulls his hand back, dropping it beside his own mug.

"Except for you dying." I don't mean to sound so resentful, but after years of believing he was dead, it's hard not to let old hurts creep to the surface.

"Except for my death," he repeats and blows out a harsh breath. "I never planned for it to happen that way, Charlotte, but after you turned five, Randall began coming around again and started showing interest in you. Wanting to know if you had manifested any special gifts yet. I did the only thing I could think of to protect you. Although, I must admit the protection spell wore off a lot later than I expected."

That captures my attention and I lift my eyes from watching the swirling liquid to my dad. "Protection spell?"

He nods. "After that day when he was poking around and asking so many questions, I went to see one of the witches a few cities over. One Randall and the others hadn't gotten their hooks into yet. In exchange from keeping you hidden from them I had to agree to do some work for her. Work that was too dangerous for me to come home after every night."

"That's why everyone thought you died," I conclude, putting off the discussion of the protection spell for a minute.

"Yes. I couldn't risk accidentally bringing that stuff home with me."

"How long was the spell supposed to work for?"

My dad shifts in his seat, glancing around the room before he finally answers my question. "Until the night of your thirteenth birthday. But something happened, and I couldn't make it back in time. By the time I could you were already a senior in high school and I was sure you would've forgotten all about me by that point." He does reach for my hand then and I don't pull away. "I never stopped watching out for you, though. By the way, we're going to talk about your love of cage diving with

Sharks," he laughs and I grin. "Charlotte," he continues, his expression turning serious again. "I'm so sorry for what I did that night. For attacking you. I don't have an excuse for my actions other than I was hoping to scare you enough so that you'd want nothing to do with those four. But I can see now that I was wrong. They're nothing like my harem."

Turning my hand over in his, I give it a squeeze. "It's okay. I can kind of see why you did what you did. I mean, I would understand better if you just came to talk to me, but I get it."

Dad goes to say something but is cut off by a piercing howl loud enough to shake the house. He quickly pushes to his feet and rushes into the living room to peer out the front door at the same time the guys pour into the room from wherever they were. Dad's eyes are frantic as he turns around.

"You need to get in your cars and go. Now," he says. He pushes past the guys to get to me and plants his hands on my shoulders. "Whatever you do, stay with at least one of your guys." He lets go and steps back so he can see all of us. "You're stronger as a unit than you are apart." Another howl pierces the air before he says, "take care of my daughter." And then he races outside.

"Dad!" I yell after him, not entirely sure what's going on. Fingers curl around my bicep and then I'm being pulled towards the door and over to the garage. I try to look over my shoulder to see what's going on but there's nothing there. "Somebody better tell me what the hell's going on?"

Usually we spilt up and take two vehicles but right now we're all piled into Jagger's jeep with me in the middle and Kane and Wolf on either side.

"That howl you heard was Cerberus warning us. It seems the Elders are done waiting," Hunter says, throwing Jagger's jeep into drive and sending the tires spinning in the snow before they gain traction and shoot us forward. "We have to break the curse today."

I can't see a thing as we drive down the driveway and then the logging road that leads to the cabin. When I glance to my right and out the window across Kane, I see a black blur running beside the Jeep.

"That's Ceb," Kane says, taking my hand in his and intertwining our fingers. "He'll try to stick with us as long as he can to warn off any Dybbuk and demons, and then he'll go back to Hades."

Tears pool in my eyes at the image of my dad running out the front door and putting his life in danger once again to save mine. I swallow them back and steel my spine. My dad and Hades have taught me enough about my power that I can be prepared for anything that happens today. The Elders have fucked with enough of the people I love.

This ends now.

CHAPTER EIGHTEEN

WE'RE JUST PASSING the school when Hunter slams on the breaks, making the tires squeal and pitching us forward. Thank fuck for seat belts. Kane and I make sure Arlo's okay but when we lift our heads to see what made Hunter slams on the breaks, the entire car stops breathing.

"How did they–" I'm not even sure how to finish that sentence.

Standing like a hoard in front of us are a bunch of ugly looking demons. No, I guess that's not fair since demons don't really have a specific look about them. They're more just shapeless beings with glowing yellow eyes. It's the feeling you get when they're around that gives away their evil nature.

We've barely had time to process what we're seeing when a black blur appears seemingly out of nowhere and plows straight through the middle of the group, followed by the Scorpion man. When I catch a glance at Hades behind them, I no longer have any questions.

"Isn't that the aqra-whatever-what-ever?" Arlo asks, her eyes focused on the scene ahead of us.

"It is," Kane answers.

"But I thought they were just sent to warn travelers?" Arlo questions.

"When Hades is involved, I try not to question things," I say.

The other guys agree as we all watch the two creatures take on what must be hundreds of demons. As soon as there's a break in the group, Hunter presses his foot down and the vehicle shoots forward. We barely make it into one of the parking lots before another hoard descends. This time accompanied by several Dybbuks and The Elders. A quick glance around what I can see of the campus assures me that it's relatively quiet except for the occasional student. Hopefully they're smart enough to stay far away.

The four of us come to a stop in a circle with Arlo in the middle. The three remaining Elders, keep coming until they're standing in front of us. Demons and Dybbuks surround us on all sides. In the distance I can still here Cerberus and Hades fighting off the original hoard. Ceb's growls and running paws send earthquake-like shakes through the ground every now and then.

"Hello, Charlotte Williams." James ignores us as his eyes eat up Arlo in the middle of our circle. "It's a pleasure to finally meet you. Although, I do wish it was under better circumstances."

Her fingers curl into the material at my back as she looks between Hunter and me and back to the Elders. "It's too bad I can't say the same," she snarls. Her eyes snap to the quiet one in the middle. "Adrian, or should I call you Randall?"

Randall's lips twitch and interest flairs behind his eyes. I think it's the first time in centuries that I've seen any movement cross his face.

"Mouthy. Just like your mother," he says. His voice hoarse, probably from the lack of use.

My little hell fire growls. "Leave my mother alone, you ancient piece of piss weasel."

From somewhere behind me, Jagger snorts and then chokes out a cough. No doubt from Kane elbowing him in the side.

"We're going to have to work on your comebacks, Little Lamb," I say through the bond.

She shrugs. "It's the best I could come up with on the spot."

"Maybe it's about time someone ought to teach you a lesson," Sean pipes up. His eyes narrow to slits on Arlo. "You *will* kneel before us."

I can practically hear her eyes roll in her head. So I'm not surprised when she snorts. "And maybe someone *ought* to remove the yogurt finger from your ass."

Hunter groans. "Baby, please, enough with the dick nicknames."

"He started it," she huffs, folding her arms across her chest.

I could kiss her right now. If for nothing else then the look on Sean's face. His cheeks are flaming red and I bet if he could, he would be close to catching fire.

"Enough," Randall's voice booms across the field. "We have been lenient with all of you up to now. Tell us how you were able to break the curse and unleash the gift of causality manipulation, and we might spare you the torture this time around. If you beg our forgiveness we'll even kill your pet mercifully instead of making you watch as we rip each limb from her body."

Before he's even done speaking the words, I feel all the tension bleeding out of us and into Kane standing at my back. This would usually be the time where one of us will try and talk him down from the ledge, not wanting a war to break out at a university in the middle of a city but fuck it. In fact, the more we can rile him up emotionally, the bigger the war. He's almost ready to explode. I can feel it. Just another little push.

That last push comes when one of the demon fuckers, manages to grab a hold of Arlo and disappears in a mist, only to reappear behind the Elders. The smug grins on their faces doesn't last long. I feel Kane slowly pivot to face them and then push his way between Hunter and me. The whiskey-colour of his eyes are replaced by a red as dark as a pool of blood.

"That was your biggest mistake." It's not a threat, but a promise from his mouth.

His voice doesn't sound like his now. It's deeper. Rougher. Almost other-worldly.

Randall's lips part on a silent laugh and then all hell breaks loose.

I had a feeling that it was going to come down to something like this. I mean, I had held out hope that I was wrong and we could do this without someone losing their life, but that was naive of me. I should've seen it coming, though. We all should have. There were enough clues to suggest how we could end this once and for all. Unfortunately, I think we were all just blind to it. Neither of us wanting it to be true. But here it is confirmed right in front of me. I wipe Sean's blood from my brow. Hell, even the Elders at one point had said that we were more valuable to them together and alive than we are apart. We should've put two and two together then. They were only able to wield our powers if they kept all of us alive since we were bound together even before being sent to Earth.

My gut churns with my final decision as the smell of fresh blood being spilt coats the air around us. Successfully kill one of us and the bond between us, and by association, the curse will be broken. Hypothetically. If it doesn't break the curse it'll at least weaken the remaining two Elders and give the guys enough time to figure out how to kill them. Where this played out has no consequence on it. Although, doing it here where Paul Williams was buried, made sure that we were stronger than ever. I believe we could've done this at the house or at either of the cabins and it would've worked just as well. But one of us dying was never in the plans. At least not theirs.

Cerberus growls somewhere in the field behind me as James and Randall circle me like predators circling their prey. James pulls out a dagger still encased in its sheath from his inside pocket. The silver of the blade gleams in the winter sun as he removes it from its protective casing.

"Where'd you get Death's Scythe?"

James waves off my question like it's not important. Like, Hunter hasn't been looking for it for centuries, ever since we were sent to Earth. It's only the one weapon in all of creation that can kill us along with every other being, mortal or immortal.

"You see," he says with a wicked gleam in his eye. "We could've killed any one of you all along, or all of you. But we spared your lives. You should be thanking us, not disrespecting us."

I snort, moving in a circle to keep James in my sights. I'm already outnumbered, being that he's the holder of the very thing that can kill any one being, human or not, on this field. I suspect that he hid the Scythe around the same time they realized Joseph had chosen a woman over them. It seems to me that James was prepared for everything. In all the stories I've heard about them over the last couple hundred years, is that James has anger issues.

With that knowledge in mind, I bait him more, needing his anger to overpower every other emotion. "You're delusional if you think we owe you anything other than hatred. You used us to carry out your sick games for centuries and want us to thank you? Yeah, that's not going to happen."

James scoffs but stops moving, allowing me to widen the circle to include Randall in my field of vision. "We merely did what the four of you would've been too weak to do by yourselves. You don't deserve to be called the Four Horsemen. You never did. That title belongs to us. And *only* us."

"Kinda hard to be the *Four* Horsemen if there's only two of you, though, isn't it?"

James' rage finally gets the best of him, and without thinking things through he rushes forward and pushes the dagger made of Death's Scythe into my stomach. His eyes grow wide as realization begins to sink in at what he just did. A crooked smile pulls at one corner of my lips at the same time, blood begins to run down my chin. James cries out in a rage and with a hand on my shoulder, pushes me off the blade. I fall to my knees in the once pristine, white snow that's now speckled with drops of my blood.

"What have you done?" He yells at me, his eyes frantic as they bounce between my wavering form and the blood on his dagger.

Randall staggers up beside him. His powers already depleting. "James," he whispers, clasping a hand on his shoulder.

In his haste to catch Randall before he collapses, James drops the dagger to wrap his arms around his lover and holds him up. With one last look to me, he seethes, "This isn't over."

My grin grows wider as I fall to my back in the snow, my body growing numb to the pain and the cold. My last thought before the darkness begins crowding in is, "It's already over."

Andréa Joy

CHAPTER NINETEEN

THERE'S A BLINDING light as soon as I open my eyes, making me have to close them again or risk going blind.

"Ah, he lives," comes a familiar voice. One I haven't heard in over a hundred years.

"Tron?" My voice sounds a lot rougher than usual and my throat feels like sandpaper when I try to swallow. I slowly try to open my eyes again and realize that the bright light I thought I saw is actually just the light playing off the brightness of the ceiling of the room I'm in.

"Looking kind of rough there, Wolf," Tron teases, helping me to sit up when I groan and try to push myself up.

"Never thought I would ever see the day I'd be back up here."

"Yeah well," he says while he fusses with my blanket and fluffs the pillow behind my back. He's been like this as long as I've known him. Even for the brief few years that we were together. Always the nurturing type. "Those that sacrifice themselves to save someone else generally find themselves up here." He huffs, sitting on the edge of the bed. "By the way, that was just stupid what you did. Admirable, but stupid. You had no idea that it was going to work or that that dickhead James would fall for it."

I shrug, and immediately frown when I don't feel any pain from where the blade punctured my skin. "It was a gamble I had to make," I say, lifting the blanket and peering down at my stomach. Nothing. There's no blood-soaked bandage, no stitches. There's not even a scar.

Tron giggles, and it conjures up so many memories of us laying by the waterfall for hours on end. "You forget that there's no pain or injuries up here."

"Yeah," I croak, running my fingers over the patch of skin where there should've been a scar and pushing the memories of Tron and I out. "How are they?" I force myself to ask, passed my dry throat.

His smile is sad as he regards me. "How do you think they are?"

I breathe out a slow breath and lean more fully back against the pillows.

"Come on," he eventually says, patting my hand. "The big man wants to see you and I think you're going to like what he has to say."

Nerves instantly begin to churn my stomach as I follow Tron down the opulent, white marble hallway and then up a curved staircase. The last time I was up here, was with Hunter, Kane, and Jagger when we were given our task and renamed the Four Horsemen. We haven't been allowed back ever since we were cursed. Even though it wasn't our fault. Although, I guess we always did have a choice. Once we were cursed, we could've chosen to sacrifice ourselves instead of obeying every command the Elders demanded. I wouldn't say we took the easy way out either. What we did for those centuries was survive. We did what we had to do to make it to where we are now, and I don't give a fuck what anyone says, it took a lot of courage for us to survive for as long as we did. And to endure all the torture we did at the hands of James, Sean, and Randall.

Tron shows me into an office that looks like it belongs in a corner office of a high rise building in some swanky down-town district. He pats me on the shoulder and then leaves me locked in here while he steps out and closes the door behind him. Part of me is tempted to follow him and hide out there for as long as I can, but even as I think it, I know it's no use.

"Don't look so scared," He chuckles, standing up from the white leather high-backed chair and walking over to the wet bar on the far side of the room. He doesn't look like he's aged a day. Which I guess isn't too surprising for someone who created the world. Literally. "Wine?" He asks, holding out an already half-filled glass of red wine.

"Thank you." I take the glasses from his finger and sip on it leisurely. "I'm a little surprised that I woke up here and not…" I trail off and wave my hand in the air.

"With Hades?"

"Well, yeah."

His pearl, silk suit moves elegantly with him as he goes to take a seat on the white leather sofa and gestures for me to take a seat on the one across from him.

"I have to tell you; I'm impressed with the way the four of you have handled yourselves on Earth given the circumstances you've been dealt. However, I'm most impressed with the way you've protected and guided Charlotte as she discovers who she is."

"The key to breaking the curse?" I ask, confused.

He smiles, but it's not patronizing. "She's so much more than the key to breaking your curse, Wolf. Charlotte Williams is a lot more powerful than she thinks. Then any of you think. She'll bring peace to war, health to plague, nourishment to famine, and life to death."

"The guys will be lucky to have her then." I drink down a healthy sip of my wine and swirl the remaining liquid up the sides. I'm doing anything to avoid looking at Him when He tells me that I'll have to watch the people I love the most, love each other from up here.

"…another chance."

My head snaps up at those words. Sure, I've heard him wrong. "I'm sorry?"

He chuckles, the sound light in the smaller room. "I'm going to let you go back, Wolf. You, Kane, Hunter, and Jagger will all get your wings back. You're welcome to come back home if you'd like too, but I suspect that might not be the case." He smiles knowingly. I can't help but stare at him. I must look like a moron, with my eyes almost bugging out of my head and my jaw dropped open. "Before you go, you must know that James can be very vengeful when something or someone he loves has been taken away from him. You've seen part of what can happen when Joseph chose another love over them, but I don't think any of you are ready for what will happen if he decides to avenge Sean's death." I frown but He continues. "James isn't a threat now, and he may never be, but that doesn't mean he's gone from your lives for eternity."

I open my mouth to ask Him more questions, but He pushes up to stand from the sofa, places his empty glass on the glass coffee table between us and heads for the door. He stops just before leaving and looks back at me over his shoulder, his pale eyes shining in the bright light. "Even though you're welcome home whenever you wish. I wish you a life filled with happiness and love. You all deserve it," He says and then He's gone.

CHAPTER TWENTY

ARLO

"WOLF!" I SCREAM, while a fresh round of tears stream down my cheeks. I start running towards where I saw his body drop, but I lose traction on the icy sidewalk and go down hard on my ass.

"Arlo!" Both Hunter and Kane call out behind me and then two sets of hands are curling around my arms and pulling me up. The four of us barely managed to sedate Chaos and destroy the army of Dybbuks and demons the Elders brought with them. We mostly have Hades to thank for showing-ing up at the last minute and jumping in to defend us. I was so relieved that we won, that it took me a minute to realize that Wolf along with James and Randall were missing. That's when I turned around and saw James plunge a knife into Wolf's body.

I try to shrug Hunter and Kane off, my eyes still glued to the spot where Wolf lies. "Let me go!" I sob. "Wolf!" *God, no. Please no. Why does this keep happening whenever I've decided to tell them I love them.*

"Arlo," Kane takes my face between his hands and forces me to focus on him. "Baby, you have to hold on to us so we can get over there. Everything is frozen and it's too slippery. We can't carry you either. Can you do that for me?"

I hiccup a sob but somehow manage a nod. I grab a hold of one of their arms and together we traverse the black ice layer on the sidewalk. As soon as my feet hit the packed snow covering the field, I let go of them and race over to Wolf. I slip and slide and even fall to my knees once, but I force myself to get up and keep running. I do a baseball slide to Wolf's body and cradle his head to my chest.

"Wolf! Answer me, dammit!" I demand, biting off my glove and pressing a couple fingers to the pulse point in his neck. Blood drips down from the cut on my forehead to join my fingers pressed against his still warm skin. "No! This is not how this ends, you hear me!? I can't lose you. Not now. Not ever."

"Arlo," Kane whispers, falling to his knees beside me.

"He's gone, Little Lamb. We can't feel him anymore," Hunter adds, dropping to his knees on my other side. His face wet with tears.

I shake my head furiously and lean down to get closer to Wolf. "No." My voice has lost some of its force, but none of the urgency. I refuse to accept that he's gone.

"They're all dead," Jagger says, panting as he approaches us from behind. Him, Hades, and Cerberus went to check on the bodies the Dybbuks had possessed. "What's going on? Where's—" His words get cut off as he gets closer and realizes who we're all bent over. "Wolf?" The snow crunches under his boots as he makes his way to the other side of Wolf's body and goes to his knees. "You sonofabitch, this isn't funny!" Jagger's eyes begin to fill with tears and when he blinks once… twice… they start spilling over. "You asshole! You promised you wouldn't get yourself killed!" Jagger reaches for Wolf's hand and brings it to his mouth. He places a kiss to the inside of Wolf's palm and then presses it to his cheek.

I don't know how long the four of us stay kneeled beside his body. It could've been days, hours, or just a few minutes, but neither of us care. My body is so numb that not even the cold or wet snow seeping through the legs of my pants are enough to get me to move or get up. It's there, in the eerie silence in the middle of a university campus that I feel it. It starts as a barely there hum before morphing into a low vibration and growing into something that I can't ignore.

I can't keep hold of my emotions anymore and start pounding my fists into Wolf's chest. Yelling and screaming at him for lying to me. For breaking his promise. "You said you'd never leave us. You said you'd always be there!"

"Arlo!" Hunter wraps his arms around me from the side but I shrug him off and push him away.

"You're a fucking coward, Wolf! I loved you, you asshole, and you went back on your promise!"

"Charlotte!" Jagger says from across Wolf's body, his voice raised higher than I've ever heard it.

"Little Lamb. Arlo, stop," Kane puts a hand on my arm and tries to drag me away but I elbow him and pull out of his grip.

"Damn you, Wolf Thompson! I hate you! You hear me? I hate you!"

"Hunter," Jagger whispers from somewhere close, but I'm too lost in my anger and grief to care.

"I know. I see it."

"Fucking hell," Kane adds.

HUNTER

BRIGHT ORANGE LIGHT seeps out from the palms of Arlo's hands and expands to include her and Wolf. I'm too stunned to move when it begins sliding over me too. Apparently Jagger and Kane are in the same boat because when the light reaches them, they don't move a muscle either. As soon as it encases all of us, I feel it. The shift in power. If I weren't already on my knees, the sheer amount of power radiating within the light would make me fall to them. I have no doubt that whatever it is, it's stronger than the four of us were, combined. But right along with it, I feel something I haven't felt in centuries except for glimpses of it here and there, more so recently after having formed my own bond with Arlo.

I drop my chin to my chest and rest my forearms on my thighs, not completely believing what I'm seeing. Bright, pale light shines out from the tips of my fingers.

"Is this really happening right now?" Kane asks beside me in awe.

I look over to see red light coming from his. Jagger is in the same position as us with his black light cutting through the orange surrounding us. The three of us turn stunned looks on Arlo where she's still on her knees and curled over Wolf's body as sobs wrack hers. The orange light is brighter the closer it gets to her body. The euphoria doesn't last and is followed by pain like I've never experienced before. I stumble back and crab crawl away from the others and as such out of the orange light. I howl in pain as I curl in on myself and bury my head in my hands, hoping it'll stop soon. I've experienced pain at the hands of The Elders, but this is nothing like that. This is worse. It feels like something is trying to push its way out of my body and take my bones with it. I vaguely register two… three similar howls around me, but I'm too exhausted to look when the pain finally recedes.

I fall on my side in the snow and curl up in a ball, but where I expected to feel cold wetness, there's a pillowy softness. Almost like… My eyes spring open. I'm shrouded in darkness except for a little sliver of light shining through the middle of whatever has me sheltered in its embrace. When I move to sit up, it moves too allowing more light to shine through. My jaw drops as I get the first real look at my wings since before we were cursed.

In my haste to stand up, I trip over my own feet and land on my knees again with my palms braced in the snow before finally getting it together enough to push to my feet. I glance first over my right shoulder and then my left thinking that maybe I hallucinated them for a minute, but no, they're still there. Big and bright blue. The colour of the Guardians. Kane and Jagger's laughter catches my attention and I look up just in time to see them embrace as their wings fold around them in their own embrace. But it's the thing in the snow that catches and holds my attention the most. Or rather the missing thing that was laying in the snow the last time I looked.

"Wolf," Arlo breathes in shock.

His head whips around and I see the most beautiful chocolate brown eyes I've ever seen in my life. He reaches out a hand to her, but she's already running towards him. He catches her in his arms with an oof and lifts her up so she's can wrap her legs around his waist.

"You didn't think you could get rid of me that easy, did you, Little Lamb?" He says with a hand to the back of her head and his nose in her neck.

"You scared me," She sobs. "I thought we had lost you for good."

"I told you," Wolf says, lifting his face so he can see her. "I'll never leave you."

She laughs but it's mixed in with a choked sob. "I love you." She frames his face in her hands and kisses him. It looks like she pours everything she's ever felt over the last twenty-four hours into the kiss. The anger, the sadness, the pain of thinking she… we had lost him, and the love she feels for not just him but all of us.

The three of us crowd in around them but Wolf doesn't let her go and neither does she let him go. Arlo looks each of us in the eyes when she says, "I love you. All of you,"

Jagger bumps Kane's shoulder and grins. "Told you." To Arlo he says, "I love you too, Little Lamb."

I grip her face and pull her into a kiss. Wolf has to tighten his hold around her waist to keep her from falling. "I love you so much, Little Lamb."

Kane elbows me out of the way so he can take my place. "I love you, Arlo." He kisses her too, but when he pulls away, something flashes in his eyes and serious Kane is back as he takes in all the new additions. "So, we're just not going to talk about the fact that we all have wings now? Or what?" The twitch in his lips gives away his playful tease.

I curl an arm around his neck and pull him in for a noogie. "Dude! Enough," he huffs, swatting at my arms until I let him go but we're both laughing. This is the lightest I've felt in a very long time.

"Yeah, about that," Wolf says, reaching around to scratch his neck. "We've, uh, been reinstated as Guardians and are allowed to go home whenever we want." He looks to Arlo and shrugs slightly. "I guess the Big Guy was impressed with how we've handled things and my sacrificing myself for our girl didn't hurt either." Wolf frames Arlo's face with his hands and leans down to kiss her. When they eventually pull back, their breaths coming out in heavy pants, he says, "We'll need to talk about these orange wings once we're all showered and curled up on the new couch at home."

"At home?" Arlo asks, completely ignoring the fact that she has Angel wings. If it were any other girl, I would think something else was going on with them, but this is it just her way of processing everything that's happened today. Her excitement or confusion will come once the adrenaline that must be coursing through her body dissipates.

Kane drags her out of Wolf's hold and into his chest. "You didn't think we'd be letting you go back to that condo by yourself, did you?"

"See, we all voted and decided that you'll be moving in with us," Jagger adds.

I hold my breath, waiting for her reaction. At first, her brows pull down in a frown and her lips purse. My stomach drops at the realization that maybe she doesn't want to commit to us like we all thought. But then her mouth curls into a bright smile and her eyes light up.

"Yes!" She squeals, bouncing on the balls of her feet. "So much yes!"

By her reaction you'd think we asked her to marry us. An image of Arlo walking down the aisle to the four of us, the curves of her body accentuated in a white gown flashes through my mind. One by one the guys turn their attention to me with goofy smiles on their faces.

Confused, Arlo follows their gazes. "What?"

With a sigh, I pull her into my side. "We're going to talk about that wall you put up between us, but not right now. Right now," I say, leaning down to growl in her ear. "I want to be buried inside you until you scream my name."

She shivers in my arms. "Race you to the cars!"

ARLO

Three Years Later...

"**W**ELL, LITTLE LAMB,**"** Wolf says, slinging an arm around my shoulders as the server comes by with another round of drinks for the table. "How does it feel to be a university graduate?"

I grin, feeling the alcohol of the last two drinks already begin to work their way through my blood stream. It's been a crazy few years with its fair share of ups and downs. Our battles didn't end that day on the field. If anything, The Elders were the least of our worries in comparison, but it made for some interesting times and brought the five of us closer together. It's taken me all this time to come to terms with the fact that I wasn't just some key in breaking the curse. No, I was more than that. I'm their polar opposite in every way. I ground them and they make me wilder. We're opposite spectrums of the colour wheel and yet we complement each other like no one ever could or can. Some days it's still hard to believe that this is my life now.

I look around the table at all my guys, Jules and her new boyfriend, and my mom. After she learned the truth about Adrian, or Randall, she was devastated, but didn't seem at all surprised. I think deep down she knew that he wasn't who he claimed to be, but she fell for him anyway.

Hunter winks at me from across the table while Jagger leans back in his seat so he can stretch his leg out to bump against mine, and Kane rests a hand on my knee. This is our last night in Canada before the five of us hop on a plane tomorrow to go live out my dream of being a Wildlife photographer. We're starting out in Florida before moving on to Hawaii and then in July we'll be heading to Guadalupe Island. And I'll be photographing and swimming with all kinds of Sharks the entire time. I can't wait.

I always thought that my life would begin after I graduated from Queen's, but I was wrong. My life began when I met the unreal turquoise eyes of a man in the hallway of the first day of school. I lean my head against Wolf's shoulder and smile at the amount of love in this little corner of the restaurant. "Great. It feels great," I say, and let my eyes drift closed for a moment when he kisses the top of my head.

Andréa Joy

THE END.

I can't believe that's another one done! I had so much fun writing this duet. I'm so happy I chose this duet as my introduction into the world of Paranormal and Reverse Harem. I couldn't have picked better characters than these five :) This might be the end of the Four Horsemen, but it's not the end of this world. Keep an eye out for Hades book coming in 2021.

ACKNOWLEDGMENTS

Nicole and Nikki, my BSB ladies. I love you! Thank you for letting me take the idea for this duet and running with it with me.

My Alpha readers, Joy and Sarah D, you ladies are awesome. I don't think this book would've been written as fast as it had if it weren't for the two of you.

BookTok After Dark. I finally feel like I've found my tribe. *#FIACrew*

Thank you to all the readers. I realize that this duet is not something you'd usually expect from me, but I can't begin to tell you how much it means that you took a chance on it anyway. From the bottom of my heart, thank you.

Andréa Joy

ABOUT THE AUTHOR

A.J. Daniels is now writing as Andréa Joy

Andréa is a shark obsessed; beach loving girl forced to endure the long Canadian winters. When she's not writing, in a lecture at the local university, or at her big girl job, you can find her binge-watching true crime shows, *Bones*, *911 Lone Star*, *Golden Girls*, or *Friends*. Coffee is her love language.

If you enjoyed *Redeemed* please consider leaving a review on your favourite eBook retailer and Goodreads.

Sign up for my newsletter to get the most up to date information on new releases: https://bit.ly/2SQp8sk

Make sure to join my Facebook group as well: A.J.'s Naughty Angels

Andréa Joy

ALSO BY ANDRÉA JOY

The Fallen Duet
Cursed
Redeemed (Dec 15, 2020)

Famiglia Series
Dark Desire (Famiglia 1)
Dark Betrayal (Famiglia 2)
Deadly Intentions (Famiglia 2.5)
Dark Illusion (Famiglia 3)
Deadly Surrender (Famiglia 3.5)
A Famiglia Christmas
Bound To You (A Famiglia Novella)
Dark Obsession (Famiglia 4)

Twist Of Fate Series
Then There Was You (Twist of Fate 1)

Andréa Joy

Redeemed